THE JOURNEY

K.M. Dean

THE JOURNEY
Copyright© 2011 JACKK WEBB Enterprises

Printed in the U.S.A

Prologue

The road to finding love is very broad; it is full of many obstacles and stops along the way. Sometimes it may seem like the destination has been reached, but then you find you've hit a wall and have no choice but to turn around and find a much narrower path.

This is a lesson only learned by experience. It isn't learned all of a sudden or even overnight. The journey to finding love begins long before we realize we are even searching. It begins with learning to trust and love yourself, and then progresses to learning to love and trust others.

Here is a story of a girl who learned a valuable lesson. She took the leap of faith, hit the ground, and was left to pick up the pieces. Luckily that wasn't the end of her story, for no story truly ever ends.

****

CHAPTER 1

I sit in the driver's seat just waiting for him to tell me we are being foolish and that I should turn around and go back home. I glance over at him and smile nervously. He smiles back which sends a whole field of butterflies fluttering through my stomach. I try to smile back but still I have this slight nervousness about me. I don't know if it's because I'm leaving my family for the first time, or if it's because I'm afraid his family isn't going to like me. He grabs my hand reassuringly and smiles again.

"Don't worry; everything is going to be okay."

I focus my eyes on the moonlit road avoiding his stare.

"What if your mom hates me?"

"She won't she loves you already. Besides if it doesn't work out, I'll take care of you, I'll keep you safe."

Something in the pit of my stomach protests at this but I push it aside and just let myself enjoy the feeling of his love and presence.

We continue down the highway a couple of hours. My mind wonders about all that might happen once we get to Upper Lake. I glance over at Garett and see him sleeping peacefully. Where would I be had he not been there to save me? Within the last month I got into a huge fight with my mother, got kicked out, lost my job, moved in with my father, made up with my mother, quit school, and was manipulated and cast aside by my father. Things happened so quickly I was taken by surprise when Garett said he wanted me to come home with him. I can still hear his words echoing through my memory.

"Come home with me, we talked about you coming down in the summer for a visit. You have nothing left here why not leave early? You could come live with us and I can be there to help you."

I smile to myself. What had I done to deserve such love? Already he has helped me out of a relationship with his cousin before it got to abusive. He saved me from my family's emotional abuse. Ultimately he saved me from myself. Without him I would have ended up on the streets.

"What?" He asks me, sitting up in the seat staring out the windshield.

Of course he would have known that I was doing some heavy thinking, spending so much time together has taught him of my different behavior patterns. I really need to teach myself not to sigh when think.

"I don't know, thank you I guess… wow that sounds really corny, but it's true."

He just smiles and squeezes my hand.

We spend the next few hours telling stories of when we were younger and all the things we did with our families. We laugh and tell jokes then begin making up our own sentences by taking turns adding a random word to each of them. I look at the clock which resets to 11:55 every time I turn off the car. 1:30 I guess since the gas gauge doesn't work and I don't know the fuel mileage we should stop for gas again. We've made about three stops already each time only putting in about ten dollars worth. I don't know how far until we reach the next stop so I guess now is better than later.

I pull up to the first gas station we spot. It looks like the only business in the area. I get out of the car and try to prepay. Just my luck the machine won't take my card without paying inside. Of course when I try to go inside to pay all the doors are locked.

Great, the only stop for I don't know how many miles and it just happens to be closed. I calmly walk back to the car and take a deep breath before climbing back in.

"They're closed."

"Well I guess we can sit here for God only knows how long… or we can chance it and keep going until we get to the next station. It's up to you; I think we can make it."

I put my seat belt on and take another deep breath. Usually I can go to Boise and back at least three times and be fine. I should be able to get another hour or so in and be okay.

Garett smiles at me reassuringly, his brilliant green eyes sparkling in the dim moonlight. I pull out of the parking lot and try to keep myself from counting down the minutes.

Never in my life had I been so anxious to get to a gas station. The first thing to be fixed in this car will be the fuel gauge.

About ten minutes later I spot two gas stations, both across the street from one another. Happily I get out to fuel up. Again I find the machine rejects my card. I groan and look back into the car.

"I'll be right back."

Once again I find myself tugging at a locked door. What the heck is wrong with people in this state? Don't they know that there aren't very many places to stop for gas around here? The least they could do is have a machine that would actually accept debit cards when the store is closed.

I climb back into the car and take off across the street, this time without hesitation.

"Well I guess if this doesn't work out we'll have to just camp out until someone comes to open."

I just look at him and glare. He smiles back with those green eyes glistening.

"We have blankets, pillows, a back seat, and each other. Things could get a little cozy."

I laugh then get out. The wind takes my breath away.

"If it doesn't work I can get cozy in the back seat and lock you out."

I close the door smiling at his pretend hurt expression. I take my card out and insert it into the machine. Finally it asks for my pin. I quickly pump the gas then hurry back into the warmth of my car. "Thank you God for this wonderful heater."

Garett covers me with his jacket and we just sit for a few minutes while I warm up.

"If I were smart I would have warn socks and tennis shoes instead of these flip flops." I stretch my legs and arms then begin on our way again.

After a while, Garett dozes off. Everything is quiet except for the roar of the thirty one year old engine. My mind begins to wonder again.

How did I end up like this? A month ago I was at home

being the miss goody two shoes that I've always been. I had everything together, I was a premed prenursing double major at BSU; I had a boyfriend that no matter how rude he became I thought I loved. I had the support and love of my family and friends; I had a job that I never dreamed of quitting. What more could I ask for? I look over at the man next to me. When everything slowly fell to pieces I thought I was going to have to pick them up all on my own. Thank you God for sending Garett my way, thank you for sending him to love and protect me, to be the ray of light when the darkness was all around. Thank you for sending him to be my best friend and catch me when I fall. I smile to myself and know that I am loved.

Garett finally begins to stir.

"Good morning sleeping beauty, sleep well?"

"Sure, sleeping in a seat that doesn't lean back is exactly where I've always wanted to sleep. Where are we?"

"I have no idea but you've been sleeping for only a half hour or so." I struggle to keep a yawn down. It's a losing battle, my eyes water as my mouth stretches wide.

"If you get too tired we can stop and I'll drive."

"I thought you said you don't drive stick."

"No, I said I don't drive stick well. If you stop out here in the middle of nowhere when no one is behind us, I can manage it."

I think back to a conversation we had a few weeks ago. We were talking about how even though my car was so old it was still very dependable. He laughed and told me that any car could smoke mine in a heartbeat. We had ourselves a little race in the mall parking lot. It wasn't a fair win since I forfeit due to the fact that the speed limit was ten and we were going at least thirty. He laughed and said it wasn't the poor cars fault but the drivers that it didn't win. As if he could drive it better. He was so proud and bragged that it was his first street race that he had won.

He asked a few days later if he could drive my car; I don't let anyone else drive it except my mother. I don't have the heart to tell him no so I simply asked if he had his license with him. Thankfully he says he left it at home. I snap back to the present.

"Do you have your license with you?"

He grins and pulls out the small plastic card from his old worn wallet. Feeling a little relieved yet nervous all at once, I pull over to the roads shoulder. We exchange places, taking time to enjoy the break and chance to stretch. Once in the car I say a little mock prayer, crossing my fingers.

"Oh come on, I'm not that bad at driving."

I put my seat belt on dramatically." We'll see about that, just try not to kill us okay."

He gives me a playful glare. Ungracefully he floors it then drops the clutch, peeling out, spraying gravel behind us. I grab on for dear life and close my eyes.

"Oh come on, it wasn't that bad. I'll admit it was bad but hey let's look at the bright side at least we weren't in town with people staring at us."

"I wouldn't have been the one embarrassed. I'm used to people staring at my car. It's you that would have been embarrassed, you're the driver."

"Yeah but you're forgetting I'm not embarrassed that easily. It's going to take a lot more than an old car and bad driving to make me blush."

I turn slightly pink as I realize he was making fun of how easily I get embarrassed. Just the other night we were lying on his grandmas front living room floor. We were just laying there talking; he said something that made me smile. It's funny how easy it is for him to make me happy. I don't know what it is about him, I guess it could be his centered yet fun personality. He could always lighten the mood just by saying a quick witted remark, causing everyone in the room to crack up laughing instantaneously. He knew when to joke and when to be serious. I love how he stands up for me whether it's my family that's hurting me, or his own.

"Your teeth are glowing." he says just inches from my face. I cover my mouth with a blanket. "Is that good or bad?"

"Well I can tell where your face is…" he pulls the blanket back down and kisses me. Every nerve in my body

comes alive. A tingling sensation begins in the pit of my stomach and shoots down my legs, making its way all the way to my toes. His lips warm and soft over mine never become pushy or greedy as all my previous kisses had. It's as if we are the only two people in existence with all the time in the world. Slowly he pulls away, leaving my heart fluttering for more.

"I'll take it as a good thing."

If only he could see my face. I'm sure its bright red by now. As if he could hear what I'm thinking he puts his hand on my cheek and begins rubbing his thumb across my cheekbone. I reach up and place my hand on his, he smiles and I smile back, lighting the way to my lips. For the second time in my life I felt my body come alive with passion fueled by a simple sweet kiss.

CHAPTER 2

"HOLY FREAKIN BATS!!!" I jump in my seat, I must have dozed off. "What…What is it?"

Garett laughs and points at a black birdlike creature soaring through the sky."I'm not so sure that is a bat. It looks like a crow to me."

"You need your eyes checked then because that my dear is a bat."

I squint out the window trying to focus on the creatures flapping wings. I can't quite make out its features.

"See look… there's another one."

I turn my head to where he nods. This time I can see it quite clearly, feathers and all.

"Hate to break it to you but that my dear is not a bat. It has a beak and feathers."

"I saw a bat, that's my story and I'm stickin' to it."

"Whatever." I say dismissing him

"See you know it's true, you just agreed."

"Actually, whatever is what I say to get people to shut their mouths before I have to get into a stupid argument that I could easily win without even trying. I used to say it to my mom just to get her to be quiet when I didn't want to hear what she had to say, especially if she was lecturing me."

"I think all of us do that just to get them to shut up or make them think they win." I chuckle, "That, and saying okay when they lecture at you. It always made my mom mad. She would yell and say *'no, it's not okay'*. If I said okay to that she would yell some more and tell me to stop saying that."

"Hmm… maybe I should try that one of these days."

"Yeah, if you want your mom mad at you."

We both laugh then fall silent. Sure I fight with my mom sometimes, what child doesn't? just because I hate it when she is right all the time and treats me like I'm two doesn't mean I don't love her. I remember at one point she used to be my best friend. I used to go to her for everything, boy problems, girl problems, work drama, everything. Lately though, she has been trying to run my life for me. I haven't been able to confide in her without getting a lecture on how I'm making a mistake and throwing my life away. I wanted a friend to listen, not a parent to lecture. I needed someone who would tell me that it's alright to make mistakes and that it's all a part of the learning experience. Growing up I had lived a pretty sheltered life, never too far from the security of my family and friends. I never had to go out and take on the real world on my own. All my life I followed the rules carefully, at home, at school, then eventually at work. Work… even that was a joke; it was a family business that I didn't think I could ever get fired from. From the time I was thirteen I would help out with the kids, and then become a capable staff member at my mother's daycare. Day in and day out I would do the exact same thing. I'd wake up at six thirty every morning, eat breakfast, go to school, go to work, do homework and then eventually go to bed. The next day would begin and end the exact same way. I vowed that once I graduated from high school I would have enough money saved up to get my own place. I was going to move out, go to college and get a different job.

I graduated high school and began college at Boise State University, that's about all I accomplished on my list of to do's. I never got away from my family or my job; it was like a bad habit that I just couldn't break. I began to hate my job, I was so easily annoyed, I would snap at everyone. Eventually it all ran into my personal life at home. I began pushing my family away and drawing closer to Jarred, Garett's cousin. This made things even worse at home.

It's funny how moms can sense danger from miles away. Mom didn't approve of Jarred and began giving me curfews and visiting hours. I was probably the only eighteen year old that would get locked out at ten on the weekends and anytime I left on the weekdays. I began to feel like I was on house arrest; I had to say where I was going and who I was with every day.

A person can only take so much. Maybe it all would have gone differently had I spoken up sooner instead of letting it all build up until I finally snapped. Mom and I got into a huge screaming match over how Jarred was physically abusive towards his family and emotionally towards me. Finally after a long week of fighting and yelling I began to take notice that not only was he emotionally hurting me, he was beginning to get physically aggressive as well. Jarred and I had been dating for almost two months, ample time for Garett and I to become good friends. He saw that I was uncomfortable around his cousin and never wanted to be alone with him. He confronted me about it.

I began to open up to him, he became my protector. Perhaps this was the reason it was so easy for me to get attached.

"Hungry?" He asks, breaking through my reverie.

"No but we can stop if you are."

"You haven't eaten anything since before we left, are you sure you don't want anything? You know you don't have to be embarrassed to eat in front of me."

I glance out the window and see people in the car next to us staring.

"I'm not hungry. I don't eat much remember, you guys tried shoving food down my throat at your grandma's house."

"Well I worry about you. I don't want you to be afraid to eat in front of me because you're shy."

"I'm not afraid to eat in front of you, hence I ate three enchiladas last night."

He just smiles and takes the next exit ramp.

"I take it you're hungry and are going to try to make me eat too."

"No it's been two hours and we need to stop for gas."

We pull into a little town which consists of a gas station, a fast food place, a couple of other stores, and one traffic light.

"Let's just hope it stays green."

Just as the words are out of his mouth the light changes, first to amber then to red.

"If you need to we can switch places really fast."

"No thank you. I got this cookie monster rolling once I

can do it again."

"Okay, just don't hurt yourself."

Once the light changes he floors it and drops the clutch. Too slow on the draw he kills it.

"Maybe I should be more concerned for the cars well being instead of yours."

"Hahaha very funny, just have a little faith would you."

I take a look behind us and laugh as the driver gives us an annoyed look. Garett tries again this time stalling, the engine catches and we speed off.

"See no harm done."

I pat the dashboard, "it's okay poor girl, the big bad driver is done hurting you." I wink at him to let him know that I was just playing around.

"Hey it could have been worse."

We pull into the gas station, fuel up and switch places.

"Let me show you how it's done." I evenly put pressure on the accelerator and let the clutch out. The car smoothly shifts to second, third, then finally fourth.

"Show off." Garett slumps back in his seat.

Once we find our way back to the highway he points out little landmarks.

"See those hills and rocks over there? That used to be where they would go mining."

"Mining for what?"

"I don't know gold I guess."

I look out across the flat land with its golden brown grass and dirt. "Have you ever wondered what it was like for the first settlers to travel across here with their covered wagons? It must have been miserable, leaving home to settle on such barren land."

"I'm sure it wasn't that bad, hard, but not bad. Many of them probably traveled here because they were searching for a new home. Kind of like you. This drive is easier for you because it's all new. I've seen it all a million times. The only thing I had to look forward to on this trip was you.

My eyes get a little teary but I shove the emotions back.

"Now that we are halfway there, what are you looking

forward to the most?"

He gets a little smile as he closes his eyes. "My mom, I can't wait to go home and have our glass of wine together. That's our thing you know, every evening after dinner we will sit down and drink a glass of wine."

This idea of him being allowed to drink at the age of nineteen was not new to me. I knew that he drank with his family and friends when he was home as long as they stayed at the house. Even at his grandma's house he would occasionally have some beer. I didn't drink but I couldn't protest his choices, he is an adult and old enough to make his own decisions. If he wanted to drink all I could say was at least he was doing it responsibly. Only once had I witnessed him being stupid while drunk. Other than that he was the most sober drunk I have ever seen.

The next morning Garett shared with me the details of what happened after I hung up. The man in the background was yelling at Jarred. Jarred apparently was digging through an old trailer wagon that was on the side of the street. The man yelled at him telling him that it was his private property and he was trespassing. Jarred told him all that was in there was garbage anyway. The man yelled at him even more and told him to step away.

Garett, having a quite a bit of false courage, stood up to the man and asked him what gave him the authority to yell at his cousin. Harsh words were exchanged before the man went inside. Minutes passed and he came out again. This time he was dressed in a police uniform. Instead of shutting his mouth and going back inside, Garett began yelling at the officer, telling him that because he was off duty he couldn't all of a sudden change into his uniform without it being impersonating an officer. He had the guts to go over to the front door and yell at the man's wife, telling her he was going to get her husband's badge number and turn him in.

I ask if he got the badge number. He just glares at the floor and tells me they laughed at him and said to go home before they got him for trespassing and disturbing the peace.

CHAPTER 3

As I continue down the highway traffic begins to thicken and the roads become snowy.

"Granny said to stay to the left."

"But the paper says right."

"Yes but Granny has made this trip at least a hundred times. She knows what she's talking about."

I look from the paper to the road. I decide listening to someone with experience is safer than taking the advice of the paper. I get as far left as possible. After about an hour of up and down hills the highway splits and we are forced to go left.

"Now stay to the right. There are going to be some pretty steep hills and you'll need to be in the slow lane."

Sure enough when we got to the hills my foot was as far as it would go on the accelerator and we were still only going twenty five. At least we weren't the slowest vehicles in the lane. Semi trucks were going even slower. Still, it is quite embarrassing watching as the other cars flew by us.

"This slow ride is making me sleepy. I'm going to doze a little if that's okay with you."

"I don't mind. I'm not even tired anymore. I had a power nap remember."

He grabs my purple throw blanket from the back seat and puts it over his head.

"Yummm… it still smells like you."

"Well I'm glad you like it that means I don't smell bad."

Silence falls again as I continue driving. Occasionally I glance over at his purple clad figure. It seems like a lifetime ago we were standing outside the gas station, him making sure I was okay while I broke it off with his cousin. Not once did he get impatient and leave. He stood off a ways but never turned his back on me. He watched the entire thing just to make sure I was alright. Only after I convinced him that I no longer needed him so close, he hesitantly went back to wait in the car.

Jarred was pretty upset and wouldn't listen to what I had to say. He tried to blame the whole break up on his cousin. He said that I was dumping him because Garett came to town and I found that I liked him better. This made me feel a little uneasy for some reason. I knew it was far from the truth. I had written a letter to Jarred the day before, explaining my reasons for breaking up with him. I gave it to Garett and told him to give it to Jarred once he thought he was ready and willing to know the truth. I gave him permission to read it and asked him what he thought about it. He said it was basically what I just told Jarred during the breakup. That's exactly what I wanted to hear. I wanted to get it through to him and everyone else that I broke up with him because I didn't love him, he was hurting me, and he needed to grow up a bit before he could ever dream of being in a serious relationship. I wrote it as heartfelt as I possibly could. I wanted to remain friends afterward but that was all up to him. He had to get over me first before friendship could be reestablished.

Funny how things worked out in the end; He ended up hating me so much that when I got kicked out and had nowhere to go, he told his grandma to leave me on the streets because it would be too awkward for me to stay there with all that happened.

I don't really remember the fight that led to me standing on the streets at 12:00 at night. All I remember is the fear and cold I felt. I had my small throw blanket, two bags of clothes and my school stuff with me. I tried calling my dad and got no answer. I tried calling my friends and got no answer from them either. While all this was going on I was texting Garett telling him everything. This is when I found out about Jarred and his problem with me coming over. Garett said he was just being a cry baby and that he would come get me even if everyone said no. I replied by saying I didn't want to be where I wasn't welcome.

My phone began to ring. I answered it surprised to find it was Jarred calling. He said he talked to his grandma and felt bad about being stupid. After I hung up with him Garett text me letting me know they were on their way.

The next thing I know Garett comes speeding down the road in his grandmas red ford focus. He slams on the breaks, hops out, grabs my stuff and tosses them into the trunk.

"Get in" he says slamming the trunk. He gets back in the driver's side. I climb into the passenger seat thankful for the warmth. I could feel the tension between Garett and Jarred in the small space separating them.

"Thank you" was all I could manage to utter.

"Don't… you shouldn't have to be thankful. You know you're always welcome in granny's home."

Jarred just glares at me from the backseat, "If someone doesn't want you there because he thinks it's too awkward he can either leave or deal with it."

Even though he said there is no need for me to be thankful, I will always be grateful no matter what. After about a week of living with him I decided I was getting too involved with him to be living under the same roof. I called my dad and made arrangements to move my stuff over there and live with him until I was finished with school. Garett was there with me every step of the way. I couldn't believe how chivalrous he was; he stood up for me when we went back to my mother's to get the rest of my stuff. He stood up for me when Jarred found out that after only a month after our breakup I was with his cousin. I didn't mean to hurt anyone and I certainly didn't mean to cause a fight between them. Things got so bad that on our last night there Jarred text me a bunch of nasty names, Garett read all of them and then threatened to beat him up if he didn't apologize. I told Garett that Jarred could hate me if he wanted to, he had a valid reason. He told me that it wasn't my fault that Jarred was a crybaby, but still I felt somewhat guilty. The whole time Garett and I were together I felt so guilty that anytime I would invite him over I would also invite Jarred. This may not have been the smartest thing I had ever done but then again we all do stupid things to make ourselves feel better.

After about another week from the time I moved in with my dad, I found out that all the things my dad was doing wasn't done to benefit but to manipulate and used me to get back at my mom. I talked it over with Garett and told him how used and cast aside I felt. This is when he decided to take me home with him.

I feel the sun hot on my chest; we've only been out of the snowy area for a half hour but the sun feels baking hot. I reach out towards the heater and flip the knob off. Suddenly Garett throws off the blanket surprising me.

"Geez are you trying to give me a heart attack?"

"Sorry. Where are we?"

"I don't know; you missed all the snow though."

"I've seen enough snow to last me a lifetime. What time is it?"

"I don't know I'm guessing one or two."

When we reach the next town we stop once again for gas.

"This should be the last stop before we get through Yuba City."

"How much longer until we get to Upper Lake?"

"A few hours, Once we make it through Yuba city time will fly by."

As the gas is pumping I turn on my phone to check the time.

"Wow I was way off, it's only ten."

"Well then I guess we'll be home around one or two."

"Any plans when we get to your house?"

"It's your house too remember. We'll probably just unpack and hang out with the family. Why, are you still nervous?"

"A little but I'm more excited than anything."

"Good, you have nothing to worry about. My family is going to love you."

I hope so; I've never been away from my family. If his family doesn't like me, what would I do? How would I get home? I have no one but Garett out here. That in itself is scary yet calming at the same time.

"I would drive but I don't want to be a bad driver in the city, I wouldn't want to ruin your car."

"It's okay, I'll drive. I hate California traffic though.

Everyone is always rushing around; it's always go go go."

"Yeah well you have to follow their speed or you'll get pulled over."

For the next hour or so, the road begins to weave in and out of some small towns. Eventually we get to a big city. Traffic wasn't as bad as I've experienced before in California. Of course I've only been to the more touristy parts of the state. This traffic was more like Boise's except no one was following the speed limit.

We were almost out of the city when we reached an intersection.

"Which way, do I follow the curve or turn right?"

"Crap I told you Yuba City wasn't my strong point on this trip. Um I think you follow the curve."

"You think or you know? I don't want to get lost in this traffic."

"Yeah, follow the curve."

I follow his directions carefully as he looks around pointing out the familiar landmarks. Good he knows where we are, we must be on the right track.

We reach a little overpass type bridge and he watches out the window.

"Okay once we get over the bridge then what?"

He continues staring out the window completely ignoring me.

"Hello... Earth to Garett..."

He turns to look at me with a dazed expression.

"Sorry... What?"

"I need you to give me the next directions. I've never been here before; I need you to focus on where we are, not on the dirt bike race going on over there."

"Sorry, I was daydreaming about my bike I'm going to get once I pass the test."

Here we go again, he is always talking about how he has his permit but has to pass the exam to get his license. He promised me that once he got it, and a bike, he would be taking me for a ride. I'm not sure if I'm excited about this or not. Motorcycles to me seem like a death wish just waiting to happen. Of course I've been told stories of bike accidents all my life so it was pretty inevitable that I would be terrified of them.

We make it safely through the city; it's not until the traffic thins though that we both relax.

"We're almost to Williams, when we get there I'll show you where some of my family lives."

"You want to stop and say hello? I don't mind stopping."

" No its okay I get to see them all the time, besides I just want to get home and have my glass of wine with my mom."

"You really missed her didn't you?"

He just smiles. We weave our way through the small town slowing down as he points out a couple of his relatives houses. When we reach an intersection by the school he quietly chuckles to himself.

"What's so funny?"

"Nothing it's just a bunch of silly memories."

"You can tell me, I won't laugh."

"When Mitchell and I were younger, Dad used to do stupid stuff to embarrass us. This one time we were driving down this street and there were some hot girls by us. Dad stopped in the middle of the intersection, rolled down the windows and blasted the music."

I laughed but then felt a little guilty. Garett had told me about his dad's tragic accident. He told me about it when we were sitting in my car at his grandma's house while he was drinking. We weren't together yet and I was sure he didn't open up about his dad to just anyone. I listened intently, letting him know that I cared. He cried a little then claimed he had to pee. I think he was just looking for an excuse to leave for a minute because he felt embarrassed. He got back in, this time in the passenger's seat. We told more stories and drew pictures on the windshield. Once he was happy again we went back into the house to go to bed. Instead we went to the backroom and listened to music all night. This was the first night he ever said I was beautiful I laughed and told him he was only saying that because he was drunk. He grabbed my hand and told me he was the most sober drunk I would ever meet.

"Dad was always doing stuff like that to us. We always forgave him for it. We loved him more than anything."

I could see tears welling up in his eyes and didn't know what to say. We came to a little stretch in the road and I could feel the tension grow thick. I knew he was still thinking of his dad.

He points to a little parking lot driveway.

"That's where it happened." Again all I could think about was him crying in the backseat of my car as he relived hearing about his father's death.

I never had the courage to ask him how long ago it was. I figured it was fairly recent because he was still so torn up about it. I also figured he didn't go through the grieving process, he was still holding on to anything and everything he and his dad shared.

"Dad and I used to just drive around listening to music. Whenever the song changed he would ask me the title and who it was by. If I knew it he would congratulate me. It felt good to make him proud."

I still had no idea what to say so I just kept my mouth shut and listened.

"See those hills over there? Upper Lake is on the other side."

Eventually we make it to the base of the hills. They seemed to be more like huge deep green mountains than hills to me.

"Everything is so luscious over here it reminds me of a little Ireland."

"What do you mean?"

"You've seen those paintings of Ireland with the rolling hills and lush greenery? That's exactly what this reminds me of."

"Just wait until the summer time, it gets so hot everything withers and turns to a more brown color."

"Whatever happened to skipping through the grass it's so fine; don't need shoes in the summer time?" He was always singing this to me. It kind of became another private joke.

"Wait, Brown like Idaho?" Garett was always picking on how brown and dry Idaho was. I tried showing him the beauty of the mountains in our back yard and our small lake. He just laughed at me and told me it was nothing compared to the mountains and lakes in his backyard. He was right, I had never seen anything so beautiful, Idaho couldn't possibly measure up, and in fact I don't think any other place could. As I am enjoying the sights my phone begins to vibrate, signaling a text. Garett flips open my phone and views the message.

"Its Mom, she wants to know if we are almost there." He replies and awaits a response.

"She asks if we went to visit dad at the cemetery." he replies again.

"Did you want to; we can go if you do."

"No, it's out of the way, we'll go another time. We're almost there and I really want to get home."

My phone vibrates once again. I was expecting it to be from his mom again. It was my friend Alison; she just found out that I left with Garett. She said it wasn't God's plan for me and that I needed to come home. We both laugh, Garett asks her how she knows that God didn't want me to come here and start a new life. There was no reply.

Back home Alison was the person I would always confide in. She was my best church friend. I could go to her for prayer requests, advice, or even just a simple hug. Even though she is younger than me she seems to be more solid and sure of her faith. I'm ashamed to admit that it sometimes made me jealous. I loved how her entire family went to church; parents, grandparents, brothers, everyone. My parents don't "Do church". I took my brothers and cousin; I hope they will continue even though I'm gone. I'm not so sure Ashley will keep going. My uncle is usually working when service begins so she won't have a ride unless my mom takes her when she takes all the boys.

Poor Ashley, she didn't even get to say goodbye. I went over to grandmas to say goodbye to everyone, she wasn't there and wouldn't be back for a couple of days. She is my best friend in the entire world and I didn't even get to say goodbye.

"You don't regret coming with me do you?"

"No, I just wish I could have told Ashley goodbye."

"You make it seem as if you're dying. You'll see her again, I promise. We can go back and visit anytime you want. Just say the words and we'll go."

"I thought you said this is the last time you were ever taking this trip."

He smiles and tosses the blanket into the back seat.

"I guess you changed my mind. Besides this time it wasn't that bad. I had some pretty good company."

"Are you going to miss anything about Idaho?"

He thinks for a minute. "Your brothers, especially Jasper and Antony."

"Yeah, you have no one to beat up now."

"I can always beat up Sean but it wouldn't be fair, I like when they fight back, especially Antony he's tough for sixteen."

Boys will be boys. I don't see what is so fun rolling around on the ground, inflicting pain on someone else.

"We'll go visit remember, it's not like you're dying."

We begin driving uphill again and my car slows five miles below the speed limit. Suddenly a car speeds past us, then another.

"By the way California law says that you have to pull over and let everyone pass you if you have five or more cars behind you."

I take a look in my rear view mirror and count seven cars.

"Great I'm breaking the law and I didn't even know it. Why didn't you tell me that before?"

"I didn't think about it until now. I forgot you aren't from around here and don't know the laws."

I pull over into a turn out." well at least we didn't get pulled over."

"I'll be more careful and let you in on more laws when you need to know them. CHP will spot your plates and pull you over for just about anything."

"Why?"

"Because they hate potatoes."

"Hahaha, very funny."

"Idaho is famous for their potatoes. Californians hate potatoes therefore CHP will pull you over for simply having Idaho plates."

"You're lying." For some reason I couldn't tell if he was or not. People can't just get pulled over for having plates from another state could they?

I look in my mirror and decide it's time to turn out again. I turn on my signal and begin to slow down. The truck behind me continues at the same speed, switches lanes, narrowly missing us.

"Holy Crap, That's why I don't like California drivers; they have no respect for anyone else on the road. They could have run us off the road and not even thought twice about it. I can't wait to get to the house; I won't have to drive with crazy people on the road."

Garett quickly changes the subject. "See the lake?"

I try looking to where he is pointing, but have to keep my eyes on the road.

"Nope I'm a little busy driving."

My phone vibrates again. It's his mom asking us to meet them for lunch.

"Is this Upper Lake?" I ask once we get into a small town.

"No this is Lower Lake, a very scary place to stay."

"What makes it so scary? It looks like a quiet, peaceful, little town."

He points down the street at a raggedy old man carrying a wrinkled paper bag with a brown bottle sticking out of it.

"People like that are all over here. It may look like just another small town to you but if you look closely you'll notice there are all kinds of creeps here."

We pull into the parking lot and wait for his parents to arrive.

"Nervous much?"

"Very." I pull at my clothes, wrinkled and grungy from

our long ten hour drive.

"Don't be they love you already."

"Yeah but look at me. No makeup, my hairs just tossed up, I'm in sweats and feel dirty."

He hugs me and smiles. "You're still beautiful."

"Yeah a beautiful mess." I mutter to myself.

We decide to find a bathroom and wait inside. I enter the ladies room and look myself over in the mirror. Quickly I try to freshen up, straightening my clothes and hair. When all is done I still look and feel horrible but decide it's as good as it gets. I guess here goes nothing.

"Please God let them like me." I take a deep breath and leave the safety of the bathroom.

Garett's mother is a beautiful petite blonde. She is the most gorgeous woman I have ever seen in the longest time. I feel so out of place with what I'm wearing and to top it off I feel fat and ugly standing next to her. She looks a lot younger than Garett said she was. She looks as if she is only in her late twenties instead of her late thirties. It didn't help me any that she looked so comfortable yet classy in a simple small black t shirt, jeans, and boots.

Her husband in his late twenties looks tired and worn out from a long day of work.

We all sit down to eat while Garett and Melinda catch up on everything that went on while they were apart. I think Melinda could tell that I was feeling a little uncomfortable. She changes the subject and focuses on telling stories of her family members that I have heard of. I had heard plenty of stories when I was in Idaho, but these stories were different. She told about this one time Jarred was staying at their house shortly after he graduated from masters, the class he was in to become a youth pastor. He had ordered some porn on their T.V. and left them the bill. One morning after that, their youngest son Nathan went to watch cartoons and saw the porn when he turned it on.

"We had to put a lock on the T.V. If you want to watch something when no one is home or something I'll unlock it for you." Brian says then takes a bite of his hamburger.

I eat mine quietly, paying attention to the conversation. I'm only halfway finished, when they are all done. Unable to eat a bite more I wrap it up and save it for later.

Once we return to the safety of my car I let out a sigh of relief.

"See it wasn't that bad now, was it?"

Garett squeezes my hand. "The hard part is over, you can relax. I told you they would love you."

He was right, there was nothing left for me to worry about. I had met the parents; they had turned out to be even nicer than I was prepared for. They even seemed to like me so far.

"We'll stop and get gas once more and then head home."

Home, I haven't truly been able to use that particular word in at least three weeks. It was nice to be able to say and hear it again.

"Home," I smile to myself.

CHAPTER 4

I pull my old car into the driveway taking note of as many details as I can. A big yellow sign displayed that we have a restaurant as our neighbor. The front lawn is beautifully landscaped, in need of mowing but beautiful all the same. The trees are barely blooming and sprouting leaves. Wild flowers dot the little meadow on the side of the house. Never in my life had I seen nature this beautiful. Garett opens my door and takes my hand. We walk down the little rock path. I'm careful enough to walk on the small, circular stepping stones.

Instead of going straight inside, he leads me around to the side of the house. We walk a ways through the tiny meadow, stopping once we get to a little stream. Garett leans over, picks a yellow daffodil, and places it in my hand. He wraps his arms around me and gives me a brief hug.

"Welcome home." He whispers in my ear.

I smile and pretend to sniff the flower, trying to hide my blush. He takes my hand and leads me back to the front of the house where we sit on a small, dark brown, wicker bench, enjoying the sun and soft breeze.

I lay my free hand on his bare arm. His gaze falls to my hand and then to his tattoo.

"Too much sun for that is bad."

I slide my hand over the logo. I asked him about the meaning of it once. He told me it was the symbol of his favorite band, Avenged Sevenfold. He said he would never get any tattoos without meaning. The next one he wanted was a pirate ship on the other forearm. This was to represent his second favorite band, In Fear and Faith.

"I have always wanted a tattoo but was always too chicken."

"Whys that?" he asks leaning back soaking up the sun.

"I'm terrified of needles."

"That's kind of ironic don't you think. I mean, you want to be a nurse but you're scared of needles, how's that suppose to work out, wouldn't you be around them all the time?"

I roll my eyes. "It's not really the needles I'm afraid of, it's the pain. Giving blood isn't that bad for me because the pain is for a good cause. A tattoo on the other hand, well that would be for my own selfish pleasure."

"And you can't be selfish every once in a while. Come on, you can't deal with a few minutes of pain for a lifetime of pleasure?"

"What happens when I get old and wrinkled? I don't want little blobs of ink randomly spotted across my body."

He chuckles, "That's why you get it where you won't wrinkle as much, silly goose."

"Down feathers"

I love our little inside joke. I don't really know what started it. I remember he was always saying silly goose to me, it wasn't annoying, and it was actually pretty cute, especially when he would say it with a lisp. Finally one day I came up with a stupid comeback that didn't really make sense, down feathers. Because it didn't make sense it was funny, so any time after that we would say it just to be cute.

"Parents are home."

I look up and sure enough I see their silver Durango and company trailer pulling into the driveway. We both remain seated until his parents make their way down the path to the front door.

"Have you taken her and shown her around yet?"

Melinda smiles excitedly. Garett told me she would be excited to finally have another girl in the house. The only girl she ever really got to talk to at home was Sandy, the dog.

"Not yet we just got here and decided to relax. We've been stuck in the car for ten hours so we are enjoying the freedom."

"Well whenever you guys are ready make sure you show her around. You guys can stay in Adam's room for now."

"Really, he doesn't let anyone stay in there… ever. Not after the whole John and Ashley thing."

"Well I told Adam that Michelle was going to be staying in there until we get things all worked out, sleeping arrangement wise."

I had this little sense of pride come over me. This family didn't even know me yet and they were already making me feel part of the family.

"After you guys get all settled in we'll eat dinner. Brian is cooking."

"Yep I'm making spaghetti."

I had heard so much about Brian's spaghetti. I was told it was the best pasta around. I'm a big fan of pasta and Italian food in general so this was something I was defiantly looking forward to.

We enter the front door into what I'm guessing is the entry hall, slash dining room, slash living room. The area is spacious and open. The décor made of soft and dark browns, the clean hardwood floor polished to a shine reminded me of the old Chinese houses I've seen in movies. The dining room table, long and antique looking had two chairs and two benches. All the furniture came together to create a feeling of peace. The deep red futon looked comfy with its many pillows. The old painting on the wall and the antique knick knacks gave the room a touch of elegance.

We walked around the house stopping at various rooms. The kitchen and laundry room, The new bathroom, Nathan's room, Mitchell's room, Melinda and Brian's room, the old bathroom and finally Adam's room.

Adam's room, like almost all the other rooms had a clean hardwood floor, white painted cement walls, and an old bamboo covered closet. He had various knick knacks from around the world, my favorite being an old antique wooden box that looked to be a letter box from china or somewhere around Asia. There was a huge temperapedic bed, old odd furniture such as an antique television set, and a bird clock that chirps the hour.

"Mom says it stays pretty cool in here during the day and it gets freezing at night."

"That's okay I brought my quilt and comforter."

"Good, I'll bring you an extra one just in case."

I don't know why but some part of me was disappointed

when he said you instead of us. I grew up being told that it was wrong to sleep with a guy until I was married. I really didn't want to stay in here by myself.

"Where are you going to be sleeping?"

"In here if you feel uncomfortable by yourself." It's as if he read my mind.

"Actually it's not about being uncomfortable. The bed looks rather comfy. I'm terrified, it's a new place and I hate new places." I was told for so long that it is wrong but it doesn't feel wrong. Besides we are just sharing a room, not having sex.

Melinda knocks on the door. She enters carrying some emerald colored sheets and pillow cases. She leaves them for us to put on and comes back with a blanket. I unfold the massive down comforter and marvel at the red and gold intricate design.

"Wow I'm going to feel like a princess in the morning."

"Whatever happened to not being a princess?" he asks playfully bringing up yet another inside joke.

"Oh yeah, I can't be a princess I'm too little, too piccala."

"I love it when you say that especially with that fake British accent. You're so good at it. It's cute, where did you say you got that from?"

I blush; I'm still not used to being called cute, pretty, or anything of that nature.

"Princess Diaries Two. It used to be one of my favorite movies."

"Oh yeah, what's your favorite now?"

"I don't know if I have a favorite as of now. It's always changing, I think though if I did have to choose, it would be Girl Interrupted. It has Angelina Jolie, Winona Ryder, and Brittany Murphy in it. It's kind of old but I love it anyway."

"I don't think I've even heard of it." He puts the last pillow case on and tosses the pillow to the head of the bed.

"Well I guess that's another movie we're going to have to watch together."

So far we were suppose to watch Star Wars, The lord of the rings series, and the new Star Trek. Garett couldn't believe that I've never seen any of those. I don't like to watch movies by myself; usually I only watch them with Ashley but she isn't really into those kinds of movies. Most of the time, we end up having to go see, the funny cartoons, comedies, or lovey-dovey mushy movies. I break the girl stereotype; I can't stand a lot of romance movies. It's always the same, girl meets guy, they fall in love, something happens causing them to break up, they get back together after realizing they are both stupid, and have a happily ever after. The only romance books and movies that I really love are those by Jane Austen and Nicholas Sparks.

"We have the Star Trek movie if you want to watch it tonight, or some other night."

"Maybe after we get all settled in. I'm so tired I could fall asleep standing here."

"If you do you'll miss out on the amazing spaghetti."

"I'm awake." We both crack up laughing, he takes my hand and leads me back through to the living room. Nathan, Garett's little brother and his friend Drake come out of the bedroom and ask if they can go over to Drake's house. Melinda gives them permission only after they introduce themselves to me.

"You remind me of my little brothers back home." He smiles and runs away shy and embarrassed.

The next couple of hours are really hard for me. I hate being in new places, it makes me feel uncomfortable because I don't know the rules or customs of the house yet. It doesn't help that I'm very shy around new people. In this house it was more like I was the new person. I had to remind myself I'm the stranger, I'm the outsider, and I'm the newcomer. Melinda and Garett were trying their hardest though to help me feel comfortable. Talking to Melinda is like talking to Ashley. I just feel so at home with her.

"Dinners ready. Come and get it.

I stick close to Garett as if he is my strength and courage. I know that his family is nice and that I can trust them, I just need the courage to step out of my comfort zone and create a relationship faster than I usually do.

Melinda shows me around the kitchen.

"Here are the cups, bowls and plates." She says opening the cupboards above the microwave.

"Paper plates, which we usually use, are in this drawer right here." She pulls out a stack and then closes the drawer.

"If you ever get hungry just come in here and help yourself to anything you want. You don't need to be shy, you can get into anything that's in here unless it's hidden, but then you couldn't find it to have it anyway." She opens the freezer showing me the various selections of microwaveable dinners.

We dish up our plates of spaghetti and take them to the living room. I take a bite savoring the starchy goodness. Back home my favorite food was always my mom's spaghetti. I have never tasted any that has come even close to hers. Everyone else's always tastes like spaghetti O's from a can. Brian's though, wow. It was the most amazing thing I have ever tasted next to my mothers.

I finish my plate and would have gone back for seconds if only my stomach would allow it. Once everyone was done eating it's time for some family fun with the Rock Band. While Garett and Brian set the game up, Melinda got the wine flowing. I wasn't much of a drinker, in fact I hadn't had alcohol since I was younger and went through a rebellious phase and would drink occasionally with my cousin. There was only one time that I really got smashed and puked my guts out. That actually was the last time I ever drank. This was different. It was just wine what could it hurt. It's not like I was going to drink to get drunk. Melinda handed me a glass with pretty pink beads around the stem.

"She's not much of drinker mom."

Garett watches as I take my first sip of wine. I almost gag but choke it down. When it first hit my tongue it was a little bitter sweet. Once I got my mouthful I decided, that was a mistake. I don't know if it was the taste or the texture but it didn't go down smoothly. I waited for the taste to settle sweetly on my tongue before taking another small sip. This time was much better, tangy but not as harsh. This is when I learned the meaning of sipping champagne, or in this case wine.

By the time my first glass was empty the game had already begun. Melinda was on vocals, Garett drums, and Brian on guitar. The song ends and Melinda hands me the mic.

"Choose a song."

"I can't sing…" The truth is I love to sing, just not in front of people. I have four little brothers to thank for that.

"That's so not true. You can sing I heard you at grannies."

I just glare at him and take the mic, I choose a song that I'm faintly familiar with and sing as softly as I can so no one can hear me. While the song fades, Melinda refills everyone's glasses.

"By the way wine makes you a little emotional." Garett whispers to me.

"I'm not sure how it affects you but you'll feel it hit you probably once you get half of that glass down."

He was wrong it took a little longer than that, by the end of my third glass I was feeling a little buzzed. I kind of like the feeling it gave me a bold and courageous feeling. I decided to step out of my comfort zone and sing out loud. His mom congratulated me on my score of 98% and said that I sounded great. She pulled me aside and we began discussing Garett.

"He must really think you're something special. He never brings any of his girlfriends home. I met one of them, Mina. I only met her for a few seconds though."

"Really, he never brought anyone else home?" This makes things a little awkward for me. Garett walks over to us and wraps his arms around me,

"What are you two up to? Not talking about me are you?"

"That's exactly what we are doing but I guess we can't anymore now that you're listening."

He looks at his mom and smiles then spins me to face him. He pulls me closer for a dance.

"Did you know Michelle was my first dance?

His mom fakes an incredulous look.

"Really?"

"Yep. I told her that I've never danced before but she thought I was lying."

At the time, I was still dating Jarred. That was the night that I found that I really did like Garett. I had a crush on him before that but that dance officially made it clear. By then I had already decided to break up with his cousin but didn't have the heart to do it before Valentines Day. I had planned a huge surprise dance. All my friends were invited. I couldn't really cancel on them especially since they already had their dresses and dates. I spent the entire day getting ready. Hair, makeup, nails, the whole shebang.

The whole plan was that Ashley and one of my friends Alina, were going to decorate then come get ready. Once everyone was ready and waiting Alina and Garett would go pick Jarred up, blind fold him and drive him around in circles to get him lost. They would then walk him through the house and to the back deck. Once everything was ready and all the candles were lit they would remove the blindfold and everyone would begin dancing.

Things don't always go as planned. None of the guys were suppose to see any of the girls until the dance began. I was trying to get ready but it seemed like nothing was going right. The decorations weren't finished, my hair was only halfway finished, I wasn't even dressed yet, it was suppose to be windy and rainy, and no one could figure out how to get the music to play. One by one all the kinks were straightened out everything and everyone was ready except for the music so I had to fix the problem. I went upstairs thinking Alina and Garett had already left to pick up Jarred. I was a little shocked and surprised to see Garett standing in the kitchen. I got to the top of the stairs, holding my dress up so I wouldn't trip over it. I felt my face turn bright red. He was just standing there staring at me.

"What are you still doing here?"

I take notice of his outfit. It reminds me of something a schoolboy would wear to a Christian school. He tugs at his black sweater, pulling it down over his black pants.

"Um… Ashley and Alina are trying to fix the candles; they said I was to make sure you didn't go out there."

"Well can you please ask one of them to come and help me I'm a complete disaster? To top it all off I told everyone we would be starting at 6:30 which is in two minutes."

He continues staring at me with those deep green eyes of his.

"You're a woman I'm sure he'll understand if you are fashionably late. Besides once he sees you he'll forget all about the time."

I feel my cheeks flush as he continues to stare. I turn away trying not to notice how fast my heart was beating. Just then, Alina comes through the door behind him and asks for his help. He excuses himself leaving me standing there breathless, with nothing to do except go back downstairs to where all the girls are still getting ready.

"Did you see that guy up there…?"

I heard one of them say. All the other girls joined in on about how cute he was and how quiet he was. My brother's girlfriend began to laugh.

"I don't think any of you stand a chance against Michelle, I saw the way he looked at you when you went up there."

"Whatever, I'm dating his cousin and I doubt anything could ever happen between us."

"So you do like him?" Another girl asks curiously.

"I never said that, and no I don't like him, I'm taken remember."

I had to keep telling myself that no one but I knew that this would be one of the last happy nights for Jarred. My heart protested the moment I denied having feelings for his cousin but I just pushed the feeling aside.

"I will admit though he is good looking. He could be a model if he truly wanted to be. And the best part for you all who are close to nineteen and think he's gorgeous, he's available."

"Too bad none of us are even close to his age. You are though."

"I'm almost 18 and very available. Michelle on the other hand is taken as she has said many times." Alina says coming through the door.

"Help me with my makeup please?" I ask her.

She goes upstairs to get her makeup bag.

"Too bad you're taken." Chelese, my brother Antony's girlfriend playfully nudges me in the ribs. It's as if she knows my plans to break it off with Jarred.

"That's enough; nothing is going to happen between us. Please stop saying stuff like that. I'm with someone which makes even talking about it wrong."

Alina never came back so I finish my own makeup and I go back upstairs to see if I'm able to fix the music situation. Again my plans fail. Jarred is already there at the top of the stairs and knows exactly where he is.

"Whatever happened to getting him lost and waiting for me to call when we were all ready?" Ashley puts her hands up in apology.

"We have an idea though to solve the problem. Neither of you have been down there to see yet, so you both get to go down at the same time. Don't worry about the music it's all been taken care of."

Someone puts their hands over my eyes and leads me and Jarred to the back deck. . On the count of three we are both uncovered. All the way down the stairs leading to the lower patio is a trail of rose petals and candles. Once we descend the staircase we reach the concrete dance floor which is encircled with candles and scattered with rose petals. The music begins and Jarred and I share the first dance. I look over his shoulder and see Garett standing with Alina's arm looped in his, his eyes on me and his cousin. I smile and he smiles back.

After a couple of faster songs, another slow song comes on. I let my cousin dance with Jarred and tell him I'm going to get Garett to participate. He is the only one sitting out at this point.

"Hey Mr. Unsociable, want to dance?"

"Oh no, I'm fine. I don't dance."

I just smile and grab his arm.

"Everyone here has to dance, that's the rule."

I pull him to his feet and he follows me out onto the dance floor. I put my hand in his; he entwines his fingers in mine. I adjust my hand so our fingers are no longer locked between each others.

"This is how you hold hands with just anyone. The other way is for couples."

He smiles nervously and puts his hand on my back, almost on my shoulder blade. I lower it to my waist.

"I'm not very good at this, like I said I don't dance."

"That's okay I'm not very good at letting the guy lead so I guess we'll be learning something new together."

We began to sway back and forth. He is a much better dancer than his cousin that's for sure. With Jarred it was like he was trying to land a plane.

"See you're not bad at all, you're actually really good at it."

"Really… you're the first girl that I've ever danced with."

My stomach flutters and I try my hardest not to let him know how glad this made me.

"NO, no, no you're doing it wrong. Garett your feet should be on the outside of hers that way she doesn't have to spread her legs." Melinda pulls him away from me and shows us how it's done.

"That way the man has more control over where her feet go."

"You know this is our third dance and we weren't even doing it right."

Our second dance was when we went to the old eagles lodge. We originally went to hang out with my friend and listen to drunken people Karaoke but ended up dancing to the music.

"At least I don't have old perverted man staring at my butt this time. What little butt I have."

"Hey…" He gives me a little pouty face. "No more being mean to Michelle."

"Okay but no more being mean to Garett either."

He looks hurt and insulted but then smiles and poses.

"Me...Be mean to Garett, why would I do that? He's the sexiest man alive."

I push him away "you're so full of yourself." He draws me back to him and holds me close.

"That's not true, underneath I have really low self esteem remember."

I roll my eyes and he leans down to kiss me softly. As always I can feel the electricity down to my toes. A minute too soon he lets go of me.

"Songs over I guess that means it's my turn again."

"Knock em dead." He kisses me one last time then returns to the game.

Melinda comes back from her room with a small plastic tote. She opens it and shows me all kinds of neat jewelry. The last thing she pulls out is a small black box. Inside is the most gorgeous ring I have ever seen. She takes it out of the box, grabs my hand and without warning puts it on my finger.

"It was left to Garett. I have a feeling it's going to be yours one day."

I slipped the ring off easily and put it back in its box. I look over at Garett and smile as I watch him play the drums.

"You know after everything he told us about you, Brian and I half expected you two would have stopped in Nevada somewhere and gotten yourselves married."

I had no idea what to say to this. "We've only been together for two and a half weeks.

Not even that if you count the time we weren't together because of that other girl, Ashley.

There are so many Ashleys to keep track of; my cousin, Garett's cousin's girlfriend, and the Ashley.

Garett had told me a little bit about her before we got together. He said they met at church and started dating, she moved away and they eventually broke up. She found herself someone else and got pregnant. I didn't find out the whole story about her until I was talking with his grandma one night about how he dumped me for another girl.

I learned that he went to Texas to visit her, taking her a promise ring. They were dating for a while before this so it was no big deal. When he gave her the ring she freaked out, told her dad she never wanted to see him again, and that he was a crazy stalker.

Garett's flight wasn't supposed to leave for a whole week. Her father kicked him out and she wouldn't speak to him while he was there. Her sister took him in and took care of him for the rest of his stay. When he went to catch his plane their father gave the ring back to him in a little plastic bag as if it were drugs and warned him to stay away.

One night at his grandma's house he told me about how he would ask her out every day over Myspace or text. She would turn him down every single time. At first it was because she was pregnant and didn't want to embarrass him, or so she said. Even after she had her baby he would ask and she would still turn him down. It wasn't until after the baby's father left and she found out Garett was with me, that she asked him out.

I don't know what made him say yes; maybe it was because he waited for her for so long. Whatever the reason, he dumped me for her.

Even though we worked things out and are together now it still hurts to think that even for a couple of days he chose her over me.

After he broke up with me I text him, questioning his decision. I asked if he remembered what he felt the entire time he was in Texas and she didn't want to have anything to do with him. I asked if he could be sure she wouldn't ever do it again.

He told me I was taking it too hard for only being together for a couple of weeks. He said I needed to get over it, he could see if it was a couple of months but it wasn't, it was just two and a half weeks and I read too much into it. I couldn't believe he was saying that. Yeah it was only a short period of time, but when you spend every minute of that time with one person, you really get attached. I reminded him that you don't just kiss someone, more than once, and tell them they read too much into it. It just doesn't work that way.

That night at church I couldn't even look at him, I was so disappointed. I spent the entire evening trying to avoid him but couldn't help seeing him anytime I turned to talk to my cousin.

All night the only thing I could think about was how he made me feel with just a simple kiss. What I wouldn't give to have just one more. I knew this was silly and I would always want just one more.

The next afternoon he text me saying he was sorry. He said that he talked to his mom and she reminded him of all the pain he felt while he was in Texas and the worse pain he felt when he was home. He apologized and said he never should have hurt me. He asked if we could try again. I accepted with one condition, we would make it official. He agreed and said he had one condition as well; we were to take it slow. I agreed and from then on we were officially together.

"It doesn't matter how long you've been together. He loves you; everyone can see it in the way he looks at you."

I just blush and empty my fourth glass.

I wait for Garett to finish the last song of the night then go to put my pajamas on. I could feel the walls spinning around me as I walked down the hallway. I lean down to pick up my cherry spotted pants and pink tank top but find my depth perception to be a little out of whack. Who knew changing could be so difficult?

"How are you feeling?" Melinda asks as I exit the bathroom.

"Spinney…" I close one eye and try to make the room slow down. "I may have had one glass too many." She laughs

"It's okay to get drunk here; you don't have to be shy. We've had people come here and get so wasted they spent the night in the bathroom."

"Well let's hope I never have to experience that myself. I'm going to head off to bed."

"Sweet dreams."

Garett follows me down the hall.

"Make sure you take her a big cup of water so she doesn't

have to get up when she is thirsty." Melinda calls to him.

"Make sure you take one for yourself too." Brian adds.

We go to the kitchen and grab two glasses of water, then head to the bedroom. He sets them both down on the nightstand then pulls me over to him. Standing toe to toe, he leans over me and presses his lips to mine.

"You okay?"

"Yeah, I'm fine just tired… and a little drunk."

I climb into bed and he pulls the blankets over me. He turns off the light, strips to his boxers and sweats then climbs over me.

"Can I ask you a favor?" I ask him brushing my hair out of my face. "Will you switch me places, I can't sleep on the edge."

He rolls over me careful not to crush me; I slide over to the wall.

"Thanks I can't sleep near doors."

He laughs, "Thanks, you would rather me get shot first."

I roll my eyes in the dark then sarcastically retort, "Yeah that's it, I'm sure the shooter would only kill one of us and leave the other as a witness."

He kisses me again, this time with a little need which creates more passion. He moves so that he is above me and kisses me a minute longer. Suddenly he pulls away.

"Dangerous." he whispers.

I smile to myself, dangerous in deed. I'm glad he is such a gentleman though; otherwise he might have had me. He lifts my head to put his arm under my neck. I roll over, laying my head on his chest, cuddling closer.

"Thank you."

"For what?" Everything is quiet for a minute before I have the courage to reply.

"For being here for me," I pat his chest, "I'm home now. I would be lost without you."

He kisses me goodnight. I turn over, he follows wrapping me tightly in his warm embrace. That night, I slept so peacefully. It was one of the rare nights I didn't wake up screaming or crying in terror. I was officially home.

CHAPTER 5

I open my eyes to the sound of birds chirping. Why do birds always have to be the creatures to wake me from pleasant dreams? I roll over to find Garett still sleeping. I remove the blanket from his face and snuggle closer. I take a deep breath, breathing in his scent. He usually always smells of axe Polaris, but now that it is all worn off I could smell his natural scent. He smelled rugged and musky, I breathed in once more savoring his warm manliness.

He opens his eyes, blinks a couple of times and then smiles.

"Good morning how did you sleep?" He kisses my forehead.

I stretch, and then pull the blanket around me tightly.

"Like a baby. I don't think I've slept the entire night through in almost five years, I don't know if I told you this but, I get really bad night terrors. Sometimes I'll wake up screaming or crying for no reason at night."

"Okay… thanks for the warning."

I take a look at the clock across the room.

"Ever since I began staying with you at your grandmas, my sleeping pattern had been so off kilter. I used to get up at five or six every morning. It's one o'clock in the afternoon."

I don't remember sleeping in this late before I met Garett.

"Well aren't we just a bunch of lazies."

Back in Idaho my brothers and I would go to all the youth group all nighters. We would stay up all night playing games and watching movies. After it ended around seven in the morning we would go home and sleep for a couple of hours. We were never allowed to sleep past nine or take naps during the day. Sleeping in until one was a luxury that I could get used to especially if I had Garett next to me. I love the feeling of his warmth and strength next to me, it made me feel less alone.

He gets out of bed, pulls on his jeans and t-shirt, slips on his socks and shoes then looks back at me.

I smile and begin singing, "If I were a boy, I'd roll out of bed in the morning, throw on what I wanted and go."

He smiles and sings back, "If I were a girl, I'd roll out of bed in the morning, take five hours getting ready then go."

I laugh and sit up making sure the blanket is covering me from my shoulders down. Some would call that being prude, I would call it being inexperienced. I was very self-conscious and not used to guys seeing me in my pajamas. It didn't help that I was a bit overweight and very sensitive about it.

"I'll let you go take a shower and dress, and then we'll go do something."

I wait for the door to close all the way before throwing on my sweatshirt. I stretch, savoring the feeling of all my muscles pulling then relaxing. I grab some of my clothes from the green storage tote in Nathan's room, then head to the bathroom.

The newly remolded bathroom was spacious and warm, it had a gray counter top, matching gray rugs, a glass shower, and a small built in space heater. After being in the cold bedroom all night, the heaters warmth is very welcoming. Anxious and excited I shower, quickly shaving, washing my hair and body, then get out. I dry myself off and look myself over in the mirror. How could a guy as thin as Garett like someone who is fat like me? I'm not obese but still at least sixty pounds overweight. I throw on my clean clothes, disgusted at my reflection.

I run a brush through my shoulder length brown hair then blow-dry it straight. After applying makeup I stand back and take another look at myself. I've been told by many people that I have a pretty face and good skin, I don't see it. All I see is an average looking girl, brown hair, brown eyes, and even brown skin. Nothing extraordinary, just plain old Michelle.

I quickly put all my toiletries in my makeup bag and store it under the counter. I put the blow dryer back in its drawer clean up my clothes and leave the bathroom. I toss the dirty clothes into a laundry basket then join the rest of the family in the living room. Brian and Garett are playing Battlefield II on the Wii. I'm not all that into video games; back home my family loved playing board and card games together. We usually had family game nights on Fridays. I would get stuck playing phase ten for hours just to end up losing dead last. Never once had I even come close to winning that game hence I hate it with a passion.

We would play other games too, most of which I also hated. I only tolerated them because I enjoyed being with my family.

Here with Garett's family was the complete opposite. I sat and watched the guys play the video game for a few hours. Once they decided to turn it off we all went outside and watched Brian mow the lawn.

"I thought you said it was illegal to pick or harm California Poppies." On the way here he had mentioned that state flowers were protected; it's illegal to pick them, even on the side of the highway.

"These are on our property; Brian mows over them all the time. If he didn't, the lawn would be patchy with long grass and orange flowers." I just smile and watch as Brian rolls over some more with the lawn mower.

Garett and I decide to go for a walk around the house. We go down the little stone path, through the carport, and enter the small gate. A huge standing swimming pool takes up half of the yard while a canopy and small boxed up garden beds take up another small portion. We walk round on a small well traveled dirt path.

"Before I went to Idaho, I would come out here and walk around this path for hours on end."

"For hours? What did you do?"

"I would just walk around and think."

We stop walking and gaze at the beautiful mountain behind the back yard. He was right; the mountains were closer, and more beautiful here than back home.

"What would you think about?"

He picks up a rock and chucks it over the fence.

"Getting out of here."

"Why?"

He begins to walk, grabbing my hand, pulling me along.

"I just wanted out."

"If you wanted out so bad, why were you so anxious to come back?"

"It was different this time."

I just look at him with a confused expression.

"This time I have you."

Again I had this feeling like I was the luckiest girl in the world. There are a billion girls out there, but he chose me. My stomach growls, interrupting my thoughts.

"I guess it's about time to eat, come on we'll have some lunch."

I hadn't even noticed I was hungry until he said something. Ever since I left my mom's house, my eating pattern has been irregular. Some days I would go all day without eating. I wasn't trying to starve myself or anything. I never thought about it, just couldn't eat. I think it was all the stress. Whatever the reason, I haven't had much of an appetite. Garett and I go inside to find Brian and Melinda already in the kitchen making sandwiches.

"I don't know what you want on yours but the mustard, Mayonnaise and everything else is in the fridge, just help yourself. There are some chips under there in that cupboard. Anything else you want just ask Garett and he'll show you where to find it."She hands me the sandwich on a paper plate.

"Thanks."

She smiles then leaves with Brian following after her.

It's funny how a person can be so nervous about meeting someone and then the next day be perfectly at home with them. Trust doesn't come very easily for me. It's hard to let people past the walls I've spent so much time and energy to build. I know that a lot of girls have been through everything I've gone through, including all that happened when I was thirteen. I vowed after that, I wouldn't let anyone that close to me again. I was never going to get hurt like that again. Garett was different, I don't know how he did it, but it's as if he tore down those walls, brick by brick, without me even realizing it was happening. I could feel the closeness we shared in the way he looks at me. Very few people know the story behind my walls, he doesn't even know. I know I should tell him, I just don't know how. What if my telling him makes him push me away? Would I be willing to risk that?

"You okay" he asks me, brushing my hair from my cheek. I smile at this small token of affection.

"Yeah, I'm fine. Why?"

"I don't know you just looked a little lost in thought."

I smile back at him again" I was just thinking of how silly I was for being so nervous about coming here."

"I told you everything would be fine, Silly Goose."

"Down Feathers." we both take our sandwiches to the dining room table and sit across from each other.

"So... what do you want to do for the rest of the day?"

"I don't know. I don't know what there is to do around here."

"Well it's a pretty small town, there's not much to do anyway."

"Well we could always go for a walk somewhere. You can show me around town."

The front door opens, interrupting our conversation.

"Mom, can Drake come over?"

Nathan, just arriving from school tosses his jacket and backpack onto the table. Melinda sits on the futon smoking pot with Brian. They explained to me the night before that it was perfectly legal in California to smoke with a prescription. Anytime they were smoking though they sent Nathan out of the room. This was another huge culture shock for me. Back home, not only was marijuana illegal, it was feared to be a horrible drug. It was explained to me that they grew it themselves and didn't put any additives in it, so it was all natural, purely THC.

Melinda and Brian both had prescriptions as did Brian's father, Joe. Joe grew it for many different patients and was allowed to grow a lot more than Brian and Melinda. Even though they grew and smoked it regularly, their children did not. Garett would occasionally have some in his mom's special brownies but very rarely did he eat them. He told me, this one time a lady made some for cancer patients and offered him some. Not knowing how strong they were he ate only a small one. Nothing happened so he ate another, still nothing so he ate some more. It wasn't long before he was having hallucinations of two monsters which kept repeatedly calling each other EEEH and AAAH. A couple of times since I've been here I heard people randomly shout out "eeeh…aaah" and crack up laughing when Garett became agitated by it.

"Finish your homework then you can go over there. You can't be in here mommy's smoking." Nathan picks up his stuff and takes it to his room. I sit and watch as Brian takes a hit then puffs out a bunch of smoke. They made sure it was okay with me before they smoked out in the living room. I told them I didn't mind, I didn't want to be rude, it was their house after all.

"I'm going to sit outside."

"Are you okay?" Garett asks me taking my hand and walking me to the door.

"Yeah I just have a headache and I'm feeling a bit light headed."

Melinda gives him a look of concern.

"Is she getting contact?"

"Yeah, we're going to sit outside for a while."

As we exit into the fresh warm air I take a deep breath and exhale.

"Sorry."

"Don't be, you'll get used to it then it won't bother you as much."

We have a seat on the wicker bench and watch the cars pass by.

"Keep your eyes on the road." Garett yells at a passing driver who was staring at us as he drove by. As I continued to watch I noticed almost every male driver stare at us as they passed.

"What the heck are they all staring at?"

"They're not used to seeing pretty women in this town."

I blush, hoping my face isn't bright red.

"Well, I'm more interested in the landscapes than the

beautiful women, or creepy guys that stare at women sitting in the front yard, with her boyfriend." I say picking up a rock then tossing it back down again.

"How about we go to the backyard, No one can stare at you back there but me."

We make our way to the backyard; stopping to watch two of their cats beat each other up playfully.

"The gray one right there, David, He's mine. The black and white one, Andrew, he looks just like his mother Larissa, everyone calls her issa though."

Andrew lies under a bush, munching on grass. David sneaks up closer to him, pauses to look around a couple of times then eventually pounces on Andrew. They wrestle for a couple of seconds before David runs off being chased by Andrew.

We continue on our way through to the backyard.

"There, no more pervs." I smile and follow him as he walks around the yard again. We stop at the back fence where he picks me a small red blossom then wraps his arms around me. We just stand staring at the area behind the fence.

"See those things right there?"

He points to little poles sticking out of the ground with small vines attached to them. We have some of those in Idaho. I've seen them on the way to my dad's house. I asked him once what they were and he said they were hops, the plants they make beer from. I know California is very famous for their wine so I take an educated guess.

"Is it a vineyard?"

He nods his head. I point to a large tan building with a blue roof. "Is that the high school?"

"Yep, unfortunately, about two o'clock every day a bunch of kids will walk home from school, cutting through that field. Not only are they disrespectful to the property, but they just hang around for about a half hour. They can be pretty noisy."

We continue walking in circles between the canopy and pool.

"When it gets hot we'll be in the pool all the time. That or on the lake."

I look in the pool and find it empty except for a small amount of water and dirt.

"It'll take some cleaning but once it's all filled up its pretty much a lifesaver."

"I don't see why everyone keeps telling me I'm going to die of a heat stroke out here. It's warm but I can still wear a sweater, it's not that hot."

"It's still pretty much winter here." Melinda says coming out of the back sliding glass door.

"It's getting to be our slow season but we still get a few sales."

It's funny to me that people in California would need to buy a fireplace. Every time before now, that I've been in California it was always in the winter time and it was always hot. I guess if I lived here year round I would think sixty five degrees was cold as well. I guess it makes sense, Brian and Melinda have had good business anyhow, whether it was the on or off season. There were all kinds of jobs to do, so I was told. They had installs, chimney sweeps, and inspections.

"Do you guys have any calls for tomorrow?" I ask curiously.

Nope but we have one Monday morning. It won't take long though it's going to be a quick sweep then we'll head back over here."

She picks up a lawn chair and moves it back to its place. She goes to check on her flower bed, pulling out a couple of weeds.

"I have a few plants inside that I want to put in here. I think I'm going to keep them in the garage a little while first though." I didn't find out until about an hour later that she was talking about the marijuana plants that were in the entryway, behind the front door.

As Melinda takes the box of plants outside, Garett and I sit in the living room on the small red futon.

"Mom used to tell Nathan that those were special tomato plants. One time we were all outside and he asked if he could have one. Everyone laughed and made him mad because he had no idea why it was so funny."

"So he has no idea what it is they are smoking?"

"Well he knows, he just doesn't understand. Mom explained to him that it is a medicine and that he doesn't need it. So he understands that mom, Brian, and a few other people smoke it, and he's not allowed to."

"He's very smart for his age. He's cute, he reminds me of my little brothers. You know, he asked me last night, since I'm with you, am I staying forever."

He stares me in the eyes and smiles leaving my cheeks feeling a little flushed. "What did you tell him?"

"I told him I'm here until you tell me to go away."

He squeezes my hand. "That's never going to happen. You'll be here forever."

I sit there staring at our hands for a minute. His fingers long and thin fit comfortably around my small hand. Suddenly he makes a strange slurping sound and moves his fingers spider like up my arms. He does this all the time to make fun of his alien looking hands, I don't think they look alien, I love his hands, they are warm and smooth, still manly but taken care of.

I grab his hand to keep him from making fun of himself. "No more picking on Garett remember."

He gives me a pouty face which cracks me up again.

"Okay no more picking on Garett."

I lean back against the arm of the futon and put my feet up underneath him, pulling my knees up to my chest.

Garett and his jokes about aliens… He was always talking about them, ghosts too. One of our first phone conversations he was telling me about this one time he was staying at his grandmas, sleeping on the couch. Out of the corner of his eye he saw something moving, when he turned his head to see what it was, he saw this orange featureless figure. Not orange like an orange peel orange but orange like a bad fake tan orange. He also told me there was a ghost living in the backroom. When he asked me if I believed in any of it, I told him I don't know. I can't disprove it but I can't prove it either. As for ghosts I believe them to be more

like demons and angels than floating transparent beings.
He told me he was more afraid of meeting an alien than a
ghost, aliens are more likely to abduct and study you. Ghosts
I defiantly believe in, I've had my fair share. Aliens though,
I'm not so sure about, they could be real, they could be fake.
I'm not going to pass judgment until I have some proof of my
own. Whichever the case I asked him politely not to discuss
them anymore. I didn't want another thing to add to my list of
fears. Ever since then he would do his little alien fingers
thing. Like most other things he did, it was pretty cute.

We sit there for a while longer. By six o'clock everyone
is done with their jobs. Brian, Melinda, Garett, and I play
rock band and get the wine flowing again. This time I'm
careful enough to have only two glasses. Garett and Melinda
go to Nathan's room, where all of our stuff is being stored for
the time being. They go through Garett's stuff putting some
of it away neatly. Melinda pulls out a stack of pornographic
magazines. This was no shocker, he pulled them out a couple
of times back at his grandmas, teasing jarred and jasper about
drooling all over the girls in them.

Melinda puts them aside. "I'm confiscating these now
that you have a girlfriend. I'll be telling your cousin not to
send you anymore."

Garett claimed he only looked at them once except for
his favorite one that he would occasionally look at. He never
bought them himself, his cousin was always sending them to
him for his birthday or other special occasions, he just never
turned him down. Melinda picks up the stack leaving one by
accident. The one left just happened to be Garett's favorite.
He picks it up and looks at me with those emerald eyes.

"Can I keep just this one? I'll put it up and never look at
it unless we are apart."

I agree and watch as he puts it in the top dresser drawer.
He zips up his duffel bag, and then tosses it with all its
contents into the closet, slides the bamboo curtain shut, and
then kisses me on the cheek. He leads me back out into the
living room where we play rock band and drink one more
glass of wine before bed.

Once settled in the big comfy bed, Garett turns the light off, strips down into his boxers and sweats then slides into bed, cradling me in his arms.

"How was your day?" he asks me kissing my temple.

"Well I did absolutely nothing except talk to the most wonderful guy all day. It went by pretty fast."

"Should I be worried about this most wonderful guy?"

I laugh and playfully elbow him. He pulls me around to face him and kisses me tenderly. I smile and lower my head.

"What… what's wrong?"

"Nothing's wrong. You have no idea what kissing you does to me."

"Oh really. You want to fill me in?"

"Uh… no it's a bit embarrassing."

After our first kiss we were texting each other about it. He told me I was only the third girl that's kissed him and that I was a good kisser. He was surprised to hear that he was only the second guy to ever kiss me and that he wasn't so bad at it himself. He asked me who the first lucky sob was and was disappointed to hear that it was his cousin. He was glad to hear though that all the kisses before his were sloppy and unpleasant.

"Tell me please…"

I sigh, "Fine… when you kiss me like that you make my toes tingle."

He smiles and kisses me again. I could feel his worm breath on mine and smell the sweet scent of wine on his breath. This made my head spin a bit. He pulls away too soon.

"What… What is it?"

This time it was my turn to be curious.

"Nothing it's embarrassing."

"So I told you. Come on tell me… Please."

"Nope"

"What, why not?"

He hugs me even closer until my face is buried gently in his chest.

"I'm a man of mystery."

"Mysteries are fun. Please tell me."

"No. It wouldn't be a mystery then now would it?"

This was my turn to take action and get him to open up to me; I pushed him far enough away to get to his lips. I kiss him, mustering up as much passion as I possibly could. He pulls away and he sighs.

"Fine…"

"Really. It worked; you're going to tell me."

All is quiet for a couple of minutes. I could see his face in the moonlight coming in through the window. He looks as if he were trying very hard to concentrate.

"It's a guy thing."

I had no idea what he was talking about so I just kept my mouth shut hoping he would explain.

He sighs again. "You have no idea what I'm talking about."

"Nope not a clue. Want to fill me in?"

As it dawns on me I remember telling him once, "Wakie Wakie eggs and Bakie." I thought it was so disgusting when he replied "Wakie Wakie, hands off snaky."

"I didn't know I had that affect on you." I smile and kiss him again. Once again he ends up above me kissing me without restraint. Again he pulls away suddenly, pulling me back into his arms. He leans in close to my ear and whispers for the second night in a row, "dangerous". I apologize and cuddle closer.

"Sometimes danger is okay."

"Not when you're not prepared."

I blush at the thought of his naked body next to mine. I close my eyes and for the second night in a row I slept the entire night through without waking up screaming or crying out in terror.

A few days pass pretty much the same way. We didn't really do much of anything different or go anywhere. We only left the house to go down the street, Melinda and Brian had to pick up something from their shop and then we went to the grocery store. When we first enter the store we head towards the deli department. Garett points up to the rafters where he sees a bird perched.

"That's really disgusting. It just goes to show how clean this store is. I mean how did it get in here in the first place?" Melinda says as we continue to walk.

Everywhere we went people were staring at me and Garett. I felt very self-conscious and a little annoyed. Some of the men walking past us would smile and wink. A couple of them had the nerve to turn their heads as we walked by.

"What the heck is wrong with men in this town? They all have a staring problem."

Melinda laughs as Garett loops his arm in mine and takes my hand.

"They're jealous…" she says turning down the next isle.

"Of what?"

"If you look at the other girls around here, they are disgusting. They aren't used to seeing pretty girls in this town."

"I wish people would stop saying that. I'm not that pretty. I mean come on, look at me."

"You look beautiful to me."

I smile at him as he spins me around in the middle of the isle. I don't know why its so easy for him to change my mind about myself; around him I feel pretty and different as if being in a new state created a whole new person.

A lady grabs a box of cat litter. The handle breaks spilling the litter all over the floor.

"It happens to all of us." Melinda says reassuringly to her.

We head to the checkout counter, we let them know about the spill then Brian pays for our items. We go back out to the Durango and load up all the groceries.

"Sean's going to be here tomorrow."

I already knew so much about Garett's thirteen year old brother. Everyone was always talking about him, especially Garett. I felt a flood of excitement at the thought of finally meeting him.

"You'll love him; he is the funniest person I have ever met." Garett says quietly in my ear. "He'll love you." I smile at this

"Let's just hope so."

"Hey everyone else loves you, he will too."

I take his word for it. As we take the highway back to the house, I spot a little college complex.

"Do you know if they have a nursing program there?" I ask Melinda.

"I don't see why not."

After this semester is over I will go check it out. I can't apply anywhere at the moment because of my current enrollment at BSU. Garett was willing to wait for me until the semester was over but I was already two weeks behind because of all the moving around. I couldn't make up any of the work and didn't see any point in sitting in a classroom only to fail anyway. I thought it kind of pointless so we left early.

"Ahh... Home sweet home." Garett climbs out his side of the car then comes around to open my door.

"Such a gentleman, thank you." He takes my hand pulling me to my feet and kisses me then lets go. I grab some groceries from the trunk and take them to the kitchen. As I turn to go back for more, Garett stops me, wrapping his arms around my waist. I smile and playfully push him away.

"Where're you going?" he says in a seductive voice.

"To help your parents." He pulls me closer not letting me go.

"Nope, you get to stay here forever."

We'll see about that, I think to myself then stand on my toes to kiss him. I press my lips tightly on his, closing my eyes and putting all my energy into it. He steps back putting his hand in his pocket.

I laugh, "That's what I thought." He smiles then pulls me to him again wanting more. This time it's my turn to be blown away. For the briefest moment he kisses me, sliding his tongue across my upper lip. He grabs my lower lip with his teeth then sucks it softly. Suddenly he walks away laughing, leaving me to just stand there staring breathlessly after him.

CHAPTER 6

Sure all his kisses and touching felt good. Don't get me wrong I loved it. The truth of the matter is though; I could live without all of it. Our relationship wasn't only physical; it was mental and emotional as well. Melinda was telling me one night that all of her kids were still virgins. She said that she raised them right and they were taught that sex is not wrong. Sex is good, as long as it is made special and not done with just anyone. All my life, I had been told that if I loved someone enough and he loved me; we would both be willing to wait until we are married. "What happens if you both wait until you're married but then when you actually have sex, you find you aren't physically attracted to one another?"

This seemed to be a valid point.

"Sex should be magical the first time. If it's with the right person it will be."

Ever since this conversation I've been thinking about it. I do love Garett, I really do. When she asked if we had done anything, I felt a little disappointed when I told her no. Deep down I knew that I really wanted to; I wanted him to be my first. I didn't want to say anything to him about it though because I thought he would be disgusted at me for even thinking about it. Luckily, I never had to bring it up. I was a little shocked when he was the first to mention it. We lay in bed, him with his arm wrapped around me, my head on his chest. I love you," I say to him lifting my eyes to his. I was a little afraid to say it, fearing it would scare him off. He kisses my forehead. "I love you too."

I close my eyes, feeling a tear dribble down my cheek. Don't say it if it's not true. I can forgive almost anything, lying will take me a lot longer to get over." Everything is quiet for a minute.

"I love you too."

I let out a sigh of relief.

"Garett?"

"Hmm…"

I hesitate a moment. "Will you do me a favor?"

"What's that?"

I pause again then whisper, "Kiss me?"

He smiles and leans in to kiss me. Slowly as if to build up the moment, he pulls me close then leans over me. He pauses to look me in the eyes then slowly lowers his lips to mine. He tastes my freshly brushed, minty mouth, slow and soft at first but then need takes over. I wrap my arm around his neck getting as close to him as possible. My toes begin to tingle and my heart races. I can feel his breath become heavy just before he breaks away. He buries his face in my neck until his breathing subsides.

"We have to be more careful." He says as my heart rate returns to normal.

"No we don't." He looks me in the eyes to see if I'm being serious.

"We can't." I feel my heart crush a little at these words. I wanted so badly to turn away to hide my pain.

"We can't…" He says again "… not tonight at least. We aren't safe."

The pain in my heart goes away when I realize he only meant we couldn't until he got some condoms.

"But…you do want to?" I ask softly. As a reply he kisses me again, this time not pulling away until we are both gasping for breath.

"We'll go to the store tomorrow if you're still sure about it. I don't want you rushing into this just because your body wants it. Sex is special to me; I don't want it to be just physical need."

I lift my hand, my small golden ring lights up, the pink heart shaped stone glistening in the moonlight. I should be disappointed in myself and feel a little bit ashamed of how much I have changed in the last couple of weeks. I push the guilt aside, my desire overpowering my thoughts.

"I couldn't agree with you more." I've owned that ring since I was fifteen. To me it wasn't just jewelry. It was a symbol of my promise, my promise to God, my church, my family and friends, my future husband, but ultimately a promise to my self. I vowed that I would keep myself pure and only lose my virginity to the man I marry. For some reason I didn't mind giving that up to Garett. I loved him with every fiber of my being. Sure I could wait until I had a marriage license in my hand but there was no 100% guarantee that I would ever even have that. Sure every girl hopes and dreams of one day becoming a Mrs. The only problem with those dreams was no one could ever tell you the name that follows that title.

I could never be guaranteed to have Garett's heart forever until the day we die. All I could be guaranteed was that I had it right at this moment. For some reason it didn't seem like enough. We had the passion for each other and the love, yes, but how long would it last? Could one person really love someone and give them their heart to treasure for a whole lifetime?

I don't know about forever. All I know is I gave Garett my heart which I would never be able to take back, no matter how hard I try. I want him to be my first and my last. It doesn't matter if things don't work out between us. He is the one I love, the one I want, the one I will treasure forever as my first. My mind is made up. Even if after he has my virginity, he decides he doesn't want me, I will always want him. I will always be there for him; he is my home, my heart, and my life now.

I fall asleep and dream of a life that I could have; being with Garett, enjoying all the love he has for me.

The entire next day I continue thinking this through. I still think this is a good idea. Anytime Garett would look at me I would have electricity pulse through my body.

"Eric, John, and Ashley are coming over." Melinda says from the bathroom where she is doing her hair and makeup.

Great, I was told by multiple people that Eric was a major ladies man. He is what my mom would call a womanizer. Now I knew why Garett was slightly irritated, already he had started drinking, he was preparing himself I guess.

"I'll warn you now though; Garett can get a little possessive."

"Well there's no need. I'll probably be sticking very close to Garett anyway. I'm not good at meeting new people remember. When I first got here I was pretty much attached to him."

Once they all arrived I made a point not to look Eric in the eyes. I didn't want to give him any reason to think I was the slightest bit interested. I am perfectly content with the man I have. I wasn't looking for anyone else. I had the best of the best.

We all began drinking, this time there was a slightly larger selection. We had, beer, lime flavored or original, and wine. I chose to go with the lime. At first it was hard to swallow, just like chugging soda, the fizz burns your throat but after the initial pain it got easier. The lime aftertaste made it a lot easier to down than the original flavor. Garett looked a little surprised to see me down my fourth and still be almost sober.

"It helps that beer doesn't make me cry."

He watches Eric watching me and wraps his arm around me possessively. I turn to face him smiling seductively.

"Don't worry, he's not even as good looking as everyone says, besides that I'm a sucker for green eyed drummers."

By the time everyone leaves I'm feeling buzzed and tired. Garett and I climb into bed the same way we do every night. He waits for me to be settled, turns off the light, and climbs in next to me. The only difference between this time and all the other nights is, when he undressed he striped to his boxers not even bothering to leave his sweats on. I wait for him to settle in then cuddle up close to him. He wraps his arms around me and tickles my feet with his.

"Guess what?"

I put my fingers over his lips and kiss him. Before the electricity could get to strong he turns me around and says, "Not tonight."

I take a deep breath and sigh. "I've thought about it all night and all day. I'm sure I want to." I say thinking he was still trying to protect me.

He laughs and smiles to himself, "That's not the

problem."

"Oh?" I ask as he kisses my temple.

"I didn't go to the store."

"Ahh... I see. It's too dangerous." I mimic his words from the previous.

He chuckles, "Very."

Instead, we find other things to do, between kisses we tell more stories of our childhood.

"Where do you want to go?" I ask trying not to sound too corny.

"Figuratively or literally?" He asks rubbing his thumb across the palm of my hand.

"Either... Both."

"Well I want to go everywhere. I would love to see anything and everything there is to see. As for where I want to go in life... I'm going to work on a ship."

This I already knew. He was going to go to school to work in the engine room or as a deckhand.

"Well with that job you'll always be traveling. You'll get to see plenty."

"Yeah, well mom doesn't like that idea." he sounded a little disappointed.

"Why not?"

"She doesn't think it will be fair to you if I'm gone all the time."

"Well you don't have to worry about that. I'm going to be a nurse remember. I'm sure I'll keep busy until you come home."

He kisses the side of my head. Everything is quiet except for the small creaking house sounds.

"Garett?" There is no reply. I turn over kissing him lightly on the cheek. "Goodnight, sweet dreams."

Since I have been with him he has always said goodnight and sweet dreams before falling asleep. Without hearing it I feel strange. Softly he moans, Goodnight... Sweet dreams."

I feel my heart swell with love as I close my eyes and drift to sleep.

I sway back and forth as the wind tosses the waves up

over the side of the ship. I run around chasing Garett's scent. Suddenly I spot him at the ship's bow. I run to him and try to touch him. The second I reach my hand out, he disappears into thin air.

I sit up in bed, my heart pounding in my ears as if I had just run a marathon. I turn over to see Garett coming back into the room carrying a cup of orange juice.

"Sorry, I didn't mean to wake you." He hands me the cup and lets me drink. I take a small sip, savoring the tanginess, and hand it back to him.

"Its okay I had a nightmare anyway. Well it wasn't a nightmare really… actually I don't even remember it."

It's funny how you can wake up from the most terrifying dream, not remembering the dream itself, yet knowing that you were scared senseless. It's even funnier when you remember the dream hours later but have no idea why you were afraid. Once Garett is settled back into the warmth of the covers, I curl up with him. He wraps the blankets around me making sure it's all tucked in.

"Goodnight… Sweet dreams" He says from the edge of my consciousness. I mutter it back and give into sleep.

"You and me forever, till the end."

I smile back at the bouquet Garett hands me. Suddenly the scene changes and we are sitting at a picnic bench with a little girl. The girl looks just like me, only she has Garett's figure and brilliant green eyes. The scene changes again, this time I'm standing back watching as the girl and Garett walk hand in hand down the street to a small yellow bus. Next we are all sitting at the dining room table. The little girl takes my hand then takes Garett's. "Please don't leave me, mommy and daddy. I love you."

"Oh sweetheart, I won't leave you but you must know; I'm not your mommy."

The little girl begins to cry then insists that I am her mother. She insists over and over until I am crying.

I open my eyes and find my cheeks wet with tears. I sit up and look around me. Thank goodness it was only a dream, a strange one at that. I lay back down, staring at Garett who is still fast asleep.

Why would I dream of such things? I better stop talking to Melinda about her future grandchildren. She was always telling me that if her sons ever got a girl pregnant she wouldn't be angry. She would be excited and proud to be a grandma. Whenever she brought up the subject I would feel awkward and have strange dreams. Sometimes the scenes were different but the child was always the same. It always ended with her trying to convince me that I was indeed her mother.

I yawn and stretch, trying my hardest not to wake Garett. My plan fails; he opens his eyes, rubbing his face with his finger tips. "What time is it?"

I look at the clock across the room. "Two. I'm going to take a shower."

Today was the day I was finally going to meet Sean. In my excitement I speed through my grooming process. Usually when I would take a shower, blow-dry my hair, and do my makeup, it would take me around forty minutes. Today it took me twenty five. I look in the mirror, feeling good about myself. I go to find Garett setting up his computer. I sneak up behind him poking him in the sides. I learned this was one of the only places he was ticklish.

"What are you up too?" I ask with a sweet tone.

"Just setting up my compooper."

"So you can geek it up on W.O.W.?"

He just smiles as he goes back to plugging in all the wires and cables.

Whenever it was just him and Jarred at his grandma's house he was constantly online playing world of war-craft. I got to watch him play a couple of times while I was over there. Usually though, when I would arrive he would put on some music and we would just sit there and talk. If we wanted entertainment, we would pull out or phones and take random pictures of each other being silly. I have this one of him trying to be gangster like with his pants droopy, a long shirt, a bandana and his hat. I tried to take the picture but he noticed I had my phone ready to snap it. He took off running leaving a blurry image on the screen. We both laughed as we noticed it looked like one of those blurry, mysterious photographs of Sasquatch.

Even though we would sit there for hour on end doing basically nothing, I was never bored. I loved Garett's company, he was, I don't know how else to explain, a charismatic person filled with life and excitement. When he told a story his whole face would light up. Just by changing the tone of his voice, he could brighten my mood as if he were in control.

"Mom and Brian are going to get Sean in about ten minutes. They want to know if we want to go."

I hadn't been anywhere except for the next town over, Lakeport. Of course I would be excited to get out of the house. Garett finishes his computer stuff, checks his mail, and then shuts it down.

Melinda walks into the room carrying a stack of Garett's clean laundry. After he finishes putting them away we head out to the car and wait for the parents.

"Can you hand me that CD case?"

Garett asks as Brian and Melinda buckle up. He spends a few minutes going through all the CD's, explaining to me the various artists and naming some of their well known songs. He finally picks one, handing it to Melinda to put in. Once the music begins, all three of them begin singing, "California Love."

Garett winks at me and continues singing. Before we even made it to the California border, he promised to sing me this song once we reached the state line. He tried to but couldn't remember most of the words. As the song comes to its end, I clap my hands.

"Now you can't say I never sang it to you."

Melinda points out her window to some trees filled with pink and red cherry blossoms. We all marvel at them for a minute before we pass them all.

"We should take her to the Japanese garden while all the trees are in bloom."

"The Japanese Garden?" It sounds pretty exotic to me.

"Yeah, you'll love it. It's very gorgeous year round but even more so when everything is blooming."

I was all up to this. I'm the kind of girl that enjoys the beauty of nature. When I was younger I wanted to be a landscape photographer. I don't know what made me change my mind, maybe I'll take it up as a hobby.

After a couple of hours we reach a small town and pull into a gas station parking lot. Garett volunteers to get his brother so his mom doesn't have to worry about an awkward moment with her ex.

He comes back with a younger boy trapped in a headlock. They wrestle a bit to get some energy out then climb into the car.

"Sean this is my girlfriend." Sean leans over his brother to smile and wave.

"His girlfriend has a name." He always introduces me like that so everyone calls me Garett's girlfriend instead of Michelle. I've been here for almost two weeks, and still Nathan calls me Garett's girlfriend.

"The names Michelle." We shake hands, and then he begins telling us some funny jokes about his school and home life. He wasn't at all what I pictured him. He was tall for his age and still had a little baby fat that he would eventually grow out of and be quite good looking. He had a friendly smile and his charm would do wonders for him in the future.

We stop at the grocery store on the way home to pick up some food and alcohol. Sean continues cracking jokes, causing me to burst out laughing every five minutes. As we walk back to the car, Sean steps in between me and Garett.

"Is she high?" He asks his brother.

"No. Why?" He replies noticing my stunned look of surprise.

"No reason, she just seems to be too happy."

"No one can be too happy. She's high on life, my own personal ball of sunshine."

He wraps his arm around my waist as we continue walking. I try not to laugh so much after this, afraid someone would accuse me of being high again.

CHAPTER 7

Late in the evening the party gets going. Sean is settled in and comfortable. Garett brings me a cup filled with some sweet smelling liquid. "What is this?" I ask him savoring the scent.

"Taste it."

I put my lips to the rim of the metal cup then slightly tip it back, taking a sip to test it.

"MMM… what is it?" I take another big gulp of the sticky sweet concoction.

"Vodka and Red Bull, Do you like it?"

I take another drink. "It certainly goes down a lot smoother."

He kisses my forehead then sits on the table next to me. I look him straight in the eyes and give him a seductive smile.

"What?" he asks taking a drink from his own cup.

"Did you go to the store?"

He puts his cup down and stands, pulling me with him.

"Nope I forgot. We can go now if you are sure."

"I'm sure but is your mom going to let us walk down to the store when we've been drinking?"

He shrugs his shoulders then checks his wallet for money.

"I guess we'll find out." he puts his wallet back in his pocket.

"Hey mom, Michelle and I are going to run to the store really fast."

"You know how I feel about you leaving the house when you've been drinking. What do you want to go to the store for anyway?"

He looks at me hesitantly. I lower my eyes a little embarrassed.

"Ummm… gum." I smile at his lame cover story.

"I don't think gum is a good enough reason. I'm sure if you want it that bad you can just ask people in this house for some."

Garett looks at Brian, "No, I have a special kind. Please

mom, we'll hurry."

Brian understands exactly what Garett is saying.

"Just let them go so they can get their condoms."

I feel my face turn bright red as Melinda's eyes grow wide.

Oh my gosh, there is no way I'm doing anything across the hall from his parents when they know exactly what we're doing.

"Well that's a different story." She laughs and makes fun of Garett's gum alibi. Garett drags me out the front door.

"Please tell me I'm dreaming, that didn't happen, and they don't have any idea."

We walk through the little meadow, cross the small creek and enter the tiny gas station. We walk around the store looking for the supplies. The lady at the front counter gives me a suspicious look.

"I'm going to wait outside." I don't even wait for a response. Mortified I step outside and wait a couple of minutes before he comes out carrying an energy drink and a small box.

"That wasn't embarrassing at all." I say sarcastically as we walk back to the house. I point to the energy drink in his hand. "Those things are so bad for you. They eat you from the inside out."

"I wasn't going to drink it. I just got it so that it didn't look like I just went in for the condoms."

"Yeah, because you went for the drink then all of a sudden decided, oh man I'm lacking the proper protection in the bedroom, Maybe I should get some more. It doesn't help that we were both went in there looking lost and embarrassed, and then I left you in there on your own. Pretty suspicious to me. What did you say to her anyway?"

"I grabbed the drink then casually went to the counter and asked if they sold any protection. I think she could tell I was nervous because she laughed and pointed to the shelf behind her. She laughed again when I told her I didn't understand the sizes. She asked me how big I thought I was. I didn't know how to answer her. I don't usually look at other guys and judge myself."

This reminds me of a little fact my brother loves to share with everyone. Every guy compares himself to others the first twenty milliseconds in the locker room.

We walk to the front door in awkward silence. Once we step into the house, Melinda and Brian are standing there waiting. Melinda cracks up laughing.

"So what flavor did you get?"

I close my eyes and head to the bedroom to hide my red face. Garett tosses the box on the nightstand. We both decide to go back out to the living room so that his parents don't suspect anything is going on just yet.

"Don't worry about anyone hearing you. Those are cement walls you can be as loud as you need."

I cover my face with my hands.

"Can we please stop talking about this?" I ask feeling completely awkward even discussing this subject with his mother.

"Okay, we're going to bed now; we'll pretend nothing is going on."

They go to their room leaving Garett and me out in the living room feeling awkward.

"It's only eight thirty; want to watch the new star trek movie?"

I jumped at the chance to make it less awkward.

"Sure if you'll bring a blanket out here." He puts the movie on then goes to get a warm blanket. I lay the futon arms down and lay on the edge, saving room for Garett behind me. He covers me up then slides in behind me, wrapping his arm around my waist. We lay there watching the movie just enjoying being together. I don't know if he truly paid any attention to what was going on in the movie, he was more busy stroking my hair and rubbing every uncovered inch of my body he could reach with his fingertips.

Before the movie reaches its end I yawn sleepily. Garett reaches for the remote and shuts everything down. He gets up and pulls me to my feet. Kissing me, he grabs my hand, and then leads me down the hall to the bedroom.

I stand at the foot of the bed and begin to undress. He turns off the light, leaving us standing in the moonlight. I stand there anxious, nervous, and excited all at the same time.

"That has got to be the sexiest thing I have ever seen." he says noting my purple boy shorts and pink tank top. I smile and watch as he slides his faded blue jeans down his hips, pulls off his sweatpants and shirt, leaving him standing in his boxers.

"I would have to agree." I say noting the small v peaking out above the spandex of his underwear. He slowly walks over to me, placing his bare feet on either side of mine. He pulls me to him and begins swaying me back and forth. He kisses my neck then begins to hum. Once his song is over he stands up on the bed, pulling me with him. He holds me steady atop the spongy mattress. Slowly he lifts his hands, running his warm fingers across my hips, my sides, my breasts, my neck, eventually pulling off my shirt. I move my arms to cover myself feeling a bit shy. We sit on the bed facing each other. He runs his fingers through my hair and kisses me, pulling me onto him. He lays me back on the bed lifting himself above me. He pulls the blankets over us to shield our naked skin from the cold night air.

He looks me in the eyes, "Are you sure you want to?" I reach up and kiss his lips, drawing him to me. He unhooks my bra and focuses his attention on my breasts. He kisses a trail from my lips to my stomach stopping once he gets to my underwear. He blows on my underwear line sending chills down my spine. He slowly removes the boy shorts and continues kissing me all the way down to my toes.

"Pretty feets." he says lingering a moment before returning to my mouth. I run my hands across his smooth chest, down his taunt stomach, to his waistband. I slide my fingers down the v of his thighs and remove his boxers. He tosses them into the heap of clothes already piled at the edge of the bed. I could feel him hard on my thigh as he lies atop me, enjoying the taste of my mouth.

He rolls away whispering, "Danger."

My body reacts with disappointment but then comes to

life as he reaches for the box on the nightstand. He opens the plastic and rolls the rubber on. Impatiently I sit up and pull him back to me. This time he kisses me without having to worry about being dangerous. He pauses only to ask me once more if I'm sure, I nod and help him into me.

All the stories I heard about sex being magical and fun were far from what I was feeling in that first moment. OI could feel him inside me but it was far from pleasurable. I could feel his warm muscle being constricted by mine. My body knew what it wanted, as did my heart and soul. My mind on the other hand was screaming for the pain to go away. I told myself that I just had to wait for a couple of minutes while my body adjusted to his. The feeling was so foreign to me but I figured I would get used to it.

"You okay?" He asks pulling me into his embrace once he finishes.

"Yeah, I'm fine." I said trying to decide if this was a lie or not. "Honestly, it hurt." I felt slightly awkward.

"I'm sorry; I didn't mean to hurt you." I pat his chest to comfort him.

"It was the first time; I was told it would hurt."

"He sighs then kisses my forehead. "You may want to go to the bathroom." I just look at him confused.

"Why?"

"You may be bleeding."

I didn't know anything about the expression popping the cherry. I've heard of it yes, but didn't really know what it meant. I offered to throw away the used condom while I was up. I went to the bathroom, quickly wrapped it in toilet paper, and then threw it away. I go pee and notice, Garett is right, there is some blood. I grabbed a tampon from my makeup bag, cleaned myself up, and then returned to bed.

"How did you know?" I ask him feeling confused yet grateful. Confused because he claimed to be a virgin, yet he knew so much. Grateful, because he saved me from the embarrassment of why we needed the sheets washed in the morning.

"I read it in a magazine once, and I have plenty of guy

cousins that like to keep me in the loop."

"Oh, well thank you. I had no idea about it."

He talks to me, reassuring me that it was magical for him. This made me happy; at least one of us enjoyed it.

I pull my purity ring off my finger and place it in his hand, wrapping his fingers around it.

"What's this?" he asks then holds it up in the moonlight. He gives me a questioning look.

"It's yours, if I wear it, it means I'm still a virgin, it would be a lie. It belongs to you now. You will always be my first."

He grabs his plain golden necklace that he always wears, from the night stand. He slides the ring on it then places it back on the bedside table. He kisses me again, causing my muscles to spasm again.

"I love you." he says, whispering in my ear.

"I love you too." I put my head on his chest, listening to the sound of his heart beating. In that moment all my walls came tumbling down. Garett was the one person I could trust with my life, my body, my soul, and most importantly, my heart.

"Garett?"

"Hmm…"

"It's funny how all this happened in this amount of time. I feel like we've always been together."

He holds me tighter as if he fears I'm going to vanish into thin air.

"I know exactly what you mean. It feels like it's been a lifetime. I'm looking forward to lifetimes to come with only you. I can't make any promises but I can promise you have my heart."

I smile and bury myself in his strong embrace.

"I love you… goodnight, sweet dreams."

"I love you too, goodnight sweet dreams." He says back. I fall asleep feeling that we are truly one.

The next couple of days my body is really tense and sore. I don't know how other women take pleasure in having sex. Sure it was fun for the guy. They didn't have their sensitive areas pulled and stretched every way with each thrust. The

first night was the most painful. The second night wasn't
as bad but truthfully it still hurt so bad I wanted to stop.

Ashley and John were staying over; John insisted that
they sleep in Adam's room. I wasn't too thrilled about this
idea but didn't say anything because Garett seemed content
sleeping out in the living room on the futon. The only true
problem I had with this sleeping arrangement was that Sean
would also be sleeping out there on his mattress on the floor.

We waited until we thought everyone was asleep before
we did anything. I felt so uncomfortable with his brother in
the room just a few feet away. Garett assured that it was fine,
Sean was a deep sleeper.

After we finished I was mortified to hear a loud yell.

"Shebang" Sean says cracking up laughing. Garett threw
a pillow across the room at him.

"I thought you were sleeping. Why didn't you say
something? Enjoy the free porn did you?"

Once Sean quit laughing, Garett rubbed my cheek
whispering to me that everything was okay.

"He couldn't see anything anyway; you were all covered
the entire time." I kept my eyes and mouth shut as I listened
to his calming voice.

Never in my life had I been so embarrassed. We move to
the floor taking advantage of the lit fireplace. I fall asleep still
thinking about how embarrassed I was. That was the worst
night of sleep I had ever had. Every two or three hours I
would wake up from the discomfort of the hard floor. Finally
at about five or six in the morning I heard Ashley and John
leave.

"Come on lets go to bed." Garett says catching me by
surprise.

Once we get into our normal sleeping positions he takes a
drink of his water that is sitting on the nightstand.

"Why were you crying last night?" He asks staring at me.
"I wasn't."

"You were. You were crying so hard but the second I put
my hand on you for comfort you stopped."

I honestly don't remember crying. I haven't done that in a

while.

"Are you sure I wasn't sleeping?"

He shrugs his shoulders.

"You were crying really hard though. I was a little scared."

"I told you about my night terrors remember. I sometimes won't even wake up. I'll cry in my sleep."

"For no reason?"

"Sometimes."

"Why?"

"I don't know. Sometimes I dream about things from my past. I don't want to talk about it right now I'm really tired and sore. I just want to go to sleep."

Thankfully he accepts that I don't feel like talking.

"Goodnight sweet dreams… I love you." This is the first time he says it first.

"Goodnight… love you sweet dreams."

I fall asleep thinking of all the pain from my past. I can't keep it a secret for long, eventually it will all have to come out. I'm not sure I can be the one to tell him. I have to though, when the time is right, I will tell him.

I have a pretty peaceful sleep. When morning comes I feel fresh and renewed. Once I hear everyone walking around out in the living room I decide it's time to get up. Garett, sensing me leave also decides to get up. I watch as he sits up and puts his necklace on. I was proud of the fact that it was the first thing he would put on in the mornings. Sometimes I would watch him stare at the ring for a couple of minutes. Other times he would randomly pull it out and fiddle with it.

"Time to go face the music."

I groan as I remember last night's show.

I shower and dress not even bothering to blow-dry or apply makeup.

When I step into the room Sean screams out "Shebang." I could feel my cheeks turn bright red.

"Be nice Sean." Melinda says putting her arm around my shoulder.

"We heard you guys put on a pretty good show last

night." Brian says causing my face to turn even redder.

"It wasn't that good; they talked through the entire thing."

Unable to stand there any longer and face the embarrassment I decided to go outside and watch the cats beat each other up.

Am never I sleep out in the living room again. The next time John and Ashley wanted to stay the night I 'm going to protect my sleeping quarters. There was no way I was going to spend another night on that hard floor or face that kind of embarrassment again. For a few nights Sean would make fun of us whenever we would say we were going to bed. Garrett yelled at him about it and they got into a fight, he won and the teasing stopped.

Things finally settled back into the normal rhythm.

I didn't mind the sex anymore; it didn't even hurt except for the first few seconds. Before I could really get the full effect, Garett would finish and we would stop. Garett would tell me that it takes a lot of energy. He would talk for a couple of minutes then pass out.

One night, after we were finished, he asked me if I would get him a cup of chocolate milk.

"Please." He pouts.

"No… you have two legs."

"Please, you're half dressed." He begs. After a few more minutes I cave in.

I quietly slide out of bed and slip out of the room. When I return, Garett is fast asleep. I set the cup on the nightstand and try to wake him. With no luck I crawl back over him, curl up and try to sleep.

"Goodnight… I love you, sweet dreams." I whisper. For the first time there was no reply.

After about an hour of tossing and turning I decide to just sit up and think. Garett turns over in his sleep, knocking over the cup of chocolate milk.

I jump out of bed and move everything out of the way.

"I don't know what to clean this up with." I shake Garett trying to get him to wake up.

"Fine, it's going to stay like this until the morning."

I climb back in bed and try to fall asleep. The last thought I have from the edge of my consciousness, is how tonight I feel like a ninety nine cent whore. He didn't even have the decency to stay awake long enough to tell me goodnight. To top it off I had another one of my dreams. This time the little girl clung to my leg, insisting that I was her mother.

CHAPTER 8

In the morning I asked Melinda what I could use to clean up Garett's milk mess. I told her about his accident, she grabbed a stack of washcloths and raced to the bedroom. She hurriedly cleaned up the sticky mess.

"Garett lift that up so I can make sure none of it went under there. If Adam finds anything wrong in here he's going to come after you."

She explained to me that Adam was an over the top neat freak. She opened his top dresser drawer, showing me neat organized stacks of military style, folded underwear. The stacks were all evenly spaced and all the same height.

"He will notice if even one thing is out of place in here. Please don't bring drinks in here anymore unless it's in a water bottle."

We both agreed then went to make some lunch. Once we had finished eating and our dishes were cleaned and put away, I was a little disappointed when he told me he was going to play World of War-craft. I couldn't really complain. He had gone this long without playing it. Before we were together, he would play it all day. I knew as well as he did that he was addicted to it. I didn't really mind that he wanted to play it; I just didn't really know what to do with myself in the meantime.

After watching him go to Nathan's room, where his computer was set up, I went to the living room expecting to sit alone on the futon. Hearing me walk across the creaky floor, Sean sits up on the mattress that's on the floor.

"Sorry I didn't mean to wake you." He rubs his eyes then gets up and sits in the rocking chair beside my seat on the futon.

"That's okay, I wasn't sleeping anyway. I was waiting for someone else to be awake."

"Where is everyone? I know Melinda was here earlier."

"I think Nathan is at Drakes and mom and Brian are out on a job."

"Sweet… so what is there to do around here while nothing's happening?"

He just shrugs his shoulders.

"We could go outside and soak up some sun,"

I look at my pasty winter arms. Usually in the summer I get really tanned. I hate winter time, I love being brown.

"Okay let's go sit outside." I head to the door.

"I'll be out in a few minutes. I'm going to go get dressed first."

I close the door behind me and sit in my favorite spot on the bench. I watch as many strange people pass by. I'm a very shy person and hate it when people stare at me, it always makes me feel awkward . I don't ever know if I'm suppose to stare back or look away, I usually end up pretending to be interested in something else so I don't draw attention to myself.

"You know there are a lot of pervs out here. I don't think Garett likes you sitting out here by yourself."

I shrug my shoulders.

"I appreciate his concern and I respect that he cares, I don't sit out here for the people that pass by. I sit out here because it's beautiful. My favorite time to sit here is sunset."

Garett and I had sat out here only a couple of times watching the sun slowly set behind the houses across the street. The beautiful blue and yellow shades turn even more gorgeous when the sun fall behind them creating shadows on the front lawn.

"Do you really love him?" His question comes from nowhere and catches me off guard.

"Of course" I say closing my eyes and smiling, trying not to think of his warm smile and sort lips.

"You better be careful, I don't want to see you get hurt."

I look at him confused.

"Careful how?"

He pats my back then leans back in the bench.

"I don't know, I just have a strange feeling. We all know that he loves you and you love him back. Maybe that's not enough."

Again I look confused.

"What are you talking about? Everything is fine between us unless you know something that I don't. What do you mean it may not be enough?"

He shrugs his shoulders then stands. "Don't get all upset or worried. I was only trying to make sure you are okay and that he's not hurting you."

I smile at him. "You are sweet, but really I'm happy, nothing is wrong between us. He treats me…as corny as this is going to sound, like a princess."

Sean smiles then begins to walk away. "Come miss sunshine, let's go to the backyard."

I really do appreciate his concern. In the few days that I've known him, he has grown on me, becoming a small piece of my heart. We go to the backyard and discuss music for a couple of hours. I was amused to learn that his favorite band was also Paramore. I was disappointed to hear, though that he learned about them from the movie *twilight*. This is one of my biggest pet peeves; Paramore had nothing to do with *twilight*. Yeah they had a couple of songs on the soundtrack but they were a band before the movie. We discussed the prettiness of Haley Williams and how we loved how she could pull off just about any hair color she wanted.

"I've always wanted to dye my hair purple." I say sarcastically.

"Did you really? That would be sweet." We both laugh and discuss more bands that we absolutely love. I don't know what it is about him, but in the past few hours he has managed to dig himself deeper into my heart.

I decide to go inside and check on Garett.

"Hey how's it going? Kill anyone lately?" I ask rubbing his shoulders. His muscles relax beneath my fingers. He rubs his eyes then stands to stretch.

"Only a few." He smiles mischievously, then leans down to kiss me.

"You about done?" I ask wrapping my arms around his neck.

"For now, I am." He kisses me again as he walks,

pushing me backwards. He kisses me until we reach the living room. We lay on the futon, he turns on the TV and we continue laying there watching a food show.

He runs his fingers through my hair, massaging my scalp. I turn to face him instead of the man eating a bug on the show.

"Hello." I say seductively as he runs his hand down my thigh. He places his other hand on my cheek.

"You're so beautiful" He whispers inches from my face.

I put my hand on his and press it tighter to my face. He leans over me pressing his lips tightly on mine. I laugh, ruining the moment, as I fall backwards. He catches me, stopping me from falling off the edge. We both crack up laughing.

"I think you two have officially lost it." Sean says coming in, sitting at the dining room table with a microwaveable dinner.

A little embarrassed I sit up, grabbing a throw pillow and hugging it to my chest. Garett also sits up, putting my feet in his lap.

"Pretty feets" he says, tickling my toe. I pull my feet away trying to hide them.

"Ewww… I have the nastiest feet in the world." He grabs my leg, running his hand down it to my foot. He holds it up checking it out.

"Nope. I love feet. You have pretty feets; they aren't all dirty and stinky. They are all soft and girly." He runs his finger from my heel to toe creating a warm electric pulse. I jump and giggle.

"That tickles, don't. I'm not used to people touching my feet."

"Well you better get use to it I love feet, especially pretty feets."

Sean stands up to leave. "You guys make me sick. If I wanted to watch all this mushy gushy stuff, I'd turn on a chick flick."

I roll my eyes and throw the pillow at him. He throws it back leaving the room before I could do anything else.

Just as we get cozy again the man on TV starts talking about eating hot peppers. Garett gets a bright idea, goes to the kitchen then comes back with a huge jar of jalapenos.

"Please don't tell me you're going to eat all of these." I watch him pull a huge one out and pop it into his mouth as if it were candy. He eats three more before the heat catches up to him. He takes a big drink of water just before the man on TV announces this is one of the worst things you could do. The water spreads the heat making it more intense.

Once the fire is gone from his mouth, he tries to hand me the jar. I look at him as if he's crazy. There is nothing in this world that could make me eat those.

"Come on sissy lawla."

Except that. I hated being called that. My brothers used to call me it because my brother Christian had a hard time saying my name when he was younger. As we got older though, it was used to mean I was weak. I give Garett a tough look then dig out five jalapenos of decent size. I pop them in my mouth, pausing to pop the stems off. I try to hide my pain as my mouth tingles with fire. Soon the pain numbs and I smile at his dumbstruck expression.

"The trick is not to chew them much. It breaks open the pores and releases the juices."

He tries eating a few more, this time only chewing them enough to swallow. He succeeds in eating eight of them without having to stop.

Once we've both had enough pain he puts the peppers away and comes back to spend more time kissing me. The peppers left my lips tingling and swollen, this didn't help the kissing process much.

The front door opens and Garett slides away from me, leaving a small gap between us. I appreciated this respect. His parents knew we were having sex across the hall from them every night; they didn't need to know that we spend our afternoons making out on the couch. We go out to the car to help carry in the groceries. As I help Melinda put them away, Garett goes back to Nathan's room to play WOW some more.

I was really disappointed when he stayed on the

computer for the rest of the day. I kept myself entertained with Sean's help, we spent hours talking and reminiscing. Secretly I thought he could be gay.

Eleven thirty rolled around and I decided I was ready for bed. I went to grab some pajamas. Garett smiles at me as I lean over the green tote.

"Going to bed?" He asks curiously. I nod. "I'll be in there in a little while." I notice a tall green cup that had orange juice in it, sitting on the desk next to him. I was pretty sure that it was a mixture of that and vodka. I just give him a small smile, change, and then head off to bed. I lie awake waiting to hear him come in. I take a look at the clock, 1:30, I'm too tired to stay up much longer so I decide to not wait up anymore and go to sleep.

I can feel the icy cold on my naked body as I run around the ship's deck. "Garett" I scream at the top of my lungs. "Garett, where are you?" I hear him softly calling back to me but I can't find him. Suddenly I feel icy fingers wrap tightly around my ankles. I grab onto the railing as the dark figure tries pulling me off the ship.

"Garett… Garett, where are you." Just as I begin falling, I open my eyes looking around in the darkness.

Immediately I jump out of bed and leave the room, looking for Garett. I see the light coming through the crack of Nathan's door. I open it and begin crying. Garett sees me, stands up and rushes to me wrapping his arms around me. As he tries to comfort me I begin sobbing even harder. He holds me at arm's length, desperately searching my eyes.

"What is it? What's wrong? Nightmare?"

I nod my head.

"I was so scared." I managed to say between sobs. "I tried reaching out for you… It was dark…You weren't there." He pulls me into his comforting arms. I bury my tear-stained face into his chest.

"I'm sorry… When you weren't there I panicked." He holds me with one arm and reaches out to shut down the computer with the other hand. I notice the time before the screen turns off, 4:00.

I felt really stupid. I had told Garett once that I am terrified of the dark. I mentioned it a couple of times back in Idaho. Even at church I wouldn't go down the hall by myself if the lights were off. You never know what's in the dark, or who. Ever since that fateful night when I was thirteen, I never went into any dark places by myself. At night I would have a nightlight on in my room. This was the first time I had been in the dark on my own in the past five years. I know it sounds stupid to a lot of people but my fear is completely rational.

Garett takes me back into the bedroom. He tucks me in and whispers "goodnight… I love you, sweet dreams."

I whisper it back, swiping my tears away. He holds me until I fall fast asleep, clinging to his warmth and strength.

CHAPTER 9

The next few days go by slowly. Melinda gave me a couple of books to read while Garett played his computer game. I didn't really mind that he was playing. The problem was he would play for hours on end. He would listen to music and play, sometimes for at least thirteen hours on end. At first I didn't mind because he would include me, a couple of times he had me play. I couldn't keep the guy moving and fight at the same time. I decided to leave the playing up to the pros. It wasn't long before he began to play and shut everyone out. I didn't understand why he would lock him in the room for hours while I often sat alone reading or texting my friends from Idaho.

My best guy friend, Brenton tried to be supportive of me but it was hard for him. He still had strong feelings for me and couldn't stand to see me get hurt. Back in high school, Brenton asked me out a few times each time I turned him down, feeling bad for hurting him. Sure he was a sweet guy and all but I thought of him as a brother. Dating him would have been weird. I told Brenton of Garett's obsession with the video game. I told him how Garett wouldn't stumble to bed drunk until two or three in the morning. All he could tell me was to come home.

I stubbornly protested and told him I couldn't. I have to stay no matter what. I don't care that it hurts to be ignored after everything we've been through. All I could do is think about all the good things I've been through since I've been with Garett.

The Garett I know and love is still here somewhere. I just need to tear down the walls and find out what his problem is.

Melinda already had a talk with him. I didn't hear the conversation but I was told she let him know she was very disappointed with his behavior. One night she told me that if I truly loved him and wanted him to pay attention to me again, I would stand up for myself and say something.

We were both very drunk standing in the kitchen

discussing my relationship with him. I let her know that in my family the women usually sit back and let the men do whatever. It was so much different over here because the women were expected to take control.

"I don't know if I could be in control. I'm used to being told what to do and being protected by the men."

"Honey men can't always protect you. Sometimes they are the ones that hurt you." She has no idea how close to home she really hit.

"I know I've learned." She looks at me with a concerned look.

"Someone's hurt you before?"

I nod my head hesitantly. "When I was thirteen." I didn't want to go through all the gruesome details of the time I went to work for my great uncle.

"My uncle and his nephew."

She looks at me with tears in her eyes.

"Did you tell someone?"

I nod my head. "I was supposed to take them to court. I told them I wouldn't testify if I had to be in the same room as them. I was so afraid of them. I knew they wouldn't have been able to touch me with police all around. I just wasn't strong enough to face them again. I hoped that the pain and nightmares would eventually go away. They never did before I came here I couldn't go even one night without waking up crying or screaming. When I'm with Garett I feel safe. Like nothing Bad could ever reach me."

"Have you told Garett about this?" She asks me putting her arm around me. I shake my head and look up to find Garett standing in the doorway.

I don't know how much of this he heard.

"I'm sorry. You have no idea how badly I wanted to tell you. I just couldn't, I didn't know how to bring it up."

"Ridiculous, you have nothing to be sorry about." Melinda says letting go of me. Once it's just me and her in the room she confides to me that this also happened to her when she was three. She said that it didn't affect her as much because she was really young when it happened and didn't really understand it."

Eventually the mood picks back up and every one continues drinking. Soon it's time to go to bed; Garett and I head to the bedroom. After our good nights I ask him if he is mad at me for not telling him.

"Why would I be mad? That is something no one should have to go through, its not your fault and there's nothing you should have to explain." Feeling at peace and completely tired, I pass out in minutes.

The next day I spent the entire day reading while Garett played the game. That night I went to bed alone again. I didn't even bother waiting up this time. I knew that I would wake up whenever he decided to come to bed. Sure enough he comes in stumbling drunk. He strips clumsily then climbs in next to me. He kisses my cheek.

"Are you awake?" He whispers through the dark.

"I am now." I turn to face the wall ignoring his advances.

"I'm too tired tonight" I say closing my eyes and pulling the blankets up over me.

I take it he could tell I wasn't in a good mood. "Do you want to talk about it?"

After a couple of minutes of silence I sigh turning around to face him. "I'm sorry. I don't want to be mad at you, I really don't."

"Then what's the problem?"

"The problem? The problem is you stay on that computer all day ignoring me and everyone else. I'm left all day with nothing to do but read or talk to Sean."

"That's not true. You can always come in and talk. I include you."

I take a deep breath to insure that my tone isn't rude.

"Even when I go in there you don't talk to me. You can't hear me anyway because you always have your headphones blaring so you can't hear anyone anyway."

I didn't want him to play but I didn't want to tell him that he couldn't. I wanted him to want to be with me more than he wanted to be online. I wanted him to be more considerate and not leave me here every night wondering when he was going to stumble into bed every night, expecting me to be awake and ready for sex. I didn't want to end up having sex just to have him fall asleep on me. Of course I couldn't explain all this to him; I didn't think he would understand he would end up blaming me and my female hormones. I sigh.

"I don't care if you play it I just don't want you to play it all day and all night."

He agrees to limit his playing time then kisses me softly.

"Goodnight... I love you, sweet dreams" He whispers in my ear.

I smile and enjoy the peace between us.

"Goodnight... I love you, sweet dreams." I whisper back. Now that we have everything worked out I can relax once again in his embrace.

I'm almost asleep again when he whispers in my ear, "Mom wants to take us to see Alice in Wonderland tomorrow."

This is something I'm defiantly looking forward to.

I awake in the middle of the night to the sound of Garett moaning in his sleep. "Don't go... Please don't leave me." He cries out. I place my hand on his face and watch his expression relax. I kiss his forehead, feeling the perspiration. I wipe his face with the blanket then tuck it around him. Placing my hands on his pillow, resting my cheek on my arms, I stare at his peaceful, handsome face until I drift off to sleep again.

Once again we sleep in pretty late. Three thirty, never again was I going to sleep so late. From now on I'm going to set my alarm and be out of bed by at least ten. I spent the next hour or so getting ready for the movie and do some laundry.

As we're getting ready to leave Garett checks his MySpace. He seemed a little grumpy this morning but it was nothing compared to when we left for the theater. He was so preoccupied with his thoughts that he forgot to pay attention to the small gentlemanly tasks he would normally do. For the first time he didn't hold my hand walking me to the car He didn't open the door for me; in fact he didn't even speak to me. Once we were standing in line, I reached for his hand. He moves it leaving me grasping at empty air. Melinda gives me a look of concern,

"What's wrong? Did you guys have a fight?"

I shrug my shoulders and shake my head. "He checked his email then got all moody. I have no idea what's going on."

We finally move through the ticket line and join the line for concessions. Garett squeezes by me and gets out of line. Melinda pays for everyone's snacks and drinks then we all head towards the room showing our movie.

"I'm going to sit back here by myself. You go sit up there with them" My heart falls, did I do something to make him not want to be around me anymore? I thought we worked everything out last night.

The entire movie all I could think about was the look of disappointment on his face.

What could possibly be wrong with him? How was I supposed to make it right if he is just pushing me away? Was it something I did?

All of a sudden everyone in the theater cracks up laughing. I turn to see Sean clutching his stomach doubled over, laughing. I decide to get lost in the movie instead of worrying about Garett. There's nothing I could do at the moment anyway, hopefully once the movie is over he'll be feeling better and he'll let me know what's going on.

Before I know it the end credits are scrolling up the screen. The house lights come on and everyone begins to file out. When we reach his row, Garett steps out into the isle. I slow my walk hoping he would grab my hand, smile at me, something, anything. Instead he waits for his family to pass and walks slower. I decide not to wait for him anymore. I was the first to reach the locked Durango. I lean against the door, clutching my heart, just waiting for everyone to catch up. Once we are all in the car I just stare at Garett waiting for some kind of explanation.

He stares back with pain in his eyes. "Please tell me what's going on." I say trying to hold my tears back.

He scoots closer to me and whispers. "I got an email with

some hurtful news. I just needed some time alone to think."

He slides back over so I figured he would need some more time alone. I could handle this now that I knew it wasn't me that caused a problem.

After everyone gets back into the house, Melinda decides to make some of her special brownies. Garett pores himself a huge cup of wine and heads straight to his computer. I watch him go without complaint, figuring he just had to sort out whatever it was that was going on. I would talk to him about it later, I wasn't tired at all but decided to say goodnight anyway. I went to the room to read until Garett is ready to come to bed.

Pretty soon I hear Melinda and Brian go to bed. They were usually the last ones up so I figured everyone else was asleep. I look at the clock which reads 11:00 exactly. I'm still not tired but hope Garett doesn't stay out there too late. I really wanted to talk to him. I felt like I had to make sure he was alright. I saw a look today that I hope I never have to witness on his face ever again.

The minutes laps to hours. All of a sudden I hear Garett in the other room singing at the top of his lungs. I can't quite make out the song but he soon pauses then picks up on another song. "What the heck is he trying to do? Wake up the entire neighborhood?" I whisper to myself. I get up throwing on my pants and sweatshirt. I hurry as fast and quietly as possible to Nathan's room. I see Nathan sound asleep on his bed and Garett slumped in his computer chair with his head on the desk. I put my hand on his back and hold my tears at bay. What the heck could possibly have happened to make him hurt so badly? I pick the large cup off his desk and smell it. It looks like chocolate milk but reeks of vodka. I look around and see an empty wine glass, some empty beer bottles and cans.

"You have got to be kidding me." I say softly. "Come on Garett, let's go to bed." He tries to stand but is unable to on his own.

A tear escapes my eye as I put my arms under his armpits

and lift with my knees.

"Why are you doing this to yourself?" I ask as his knees buckle underneath him. Once I get him standing straight, I put his arm around my neck and help him move slowly to the door. I was doing most of the work for him, sliding my foot behind his pushing him forward.

"Garett, I need you to help me. I can't do this on my own. I can keep you up but you have to open the doors, or keep yourself up while I open them. I can't do both, I'm not strong enough." He lays his head on my shoulder to keep himself up as I reach one hand out to turn the knob. All that I could think was who could possibly have emailed him and what could they have said to cause him to drink like this. I was beyond terrified, all I could do besides slowly drag him down the hall, is pray that I get him to bed safely and that he would be okay through the night.

One of my friends told me once, about a friend who had died in her sleep from drinking too much. I pray that this fate would not fall on him as well.

As we shuffle our way down the hall he half whispers, half moans, "Thank you."

Tears fall from my eyes as I drag his helpless body down the rest of the hall. After what seems like an hour, I help him gently to the bed. I undress him and tuck him in. Careful not to squish or hurt him, I climb over to my side and just sit there praying and watching over him.

I thought he had fallen asleep so I let all the tears I was trying so hard to hold back roll down my face.

"That email…"

I wipe my tears feeling foolish and weak. He continues "It was Ashley. She found out about us and deleted me from her MySpace."

I felt a slight bit guilty for being happy about this. I still hurt every time I hear her name because of the time he chose her over me. At the same time I feel sorry for him. Ashley to him is like Brenton to me. I shared everything with Brenton and couldn't stand it if I was to never speak to him again. I know I should have been the jealous girlfriend towards her.

I'm not that kind of person, sure I was hurt by his choice but in the end he chose me. I will never forget that he loved her once, and I respect her for that. But moving in on someone that's already taken, Come on that's stooping pretty low. I had no idea what to say to him. All I could manage was a sincere. "I'm sorry Garett, I really am."

His breathing grows deep, I decided I'd try to sit up the entire night and watch over him, making sure he's alright.

I kiss his forehead softly and for the first time since the beginning of my new life I cried uncontrollably with a broken heart.

I stay up as long as I can, I don't even realize when my life slips into a dream.

I'm lying in a hospital bed with tubes and wires poking out of me everywhere. My friend Brenton and his fiancé stand at the foot of the bed; Garett stands next to me holding my hand. Suddenly I feel little spasms of pain as a baby pops out of me. More pop out in even intervals. I look to the foot of the bed and see Brenton and his fiancé eating the babies. I begin to cry and scream at Garett to stop them.

I open my eyes which are burning from my night of tears. I check the time 10:00. I've been asleep for at most five hours. I could feel my eyes swollen and my cheeks raw. I look at Garett and am relieved to see his chest rise and fall deeply as he breaths.

Quietly so as not to wake him I slide out of bed and leave the room. I shower and dress not bothering with the blow-dryer or makeup. I go sit outside to hang out with Sean

"Hey sis, how's it going?"

Hanging out with him so much created a bond between us. He looked up to me as an older sister; I loved him as my own brother.

"Good, how did you sleep?" He watches me as I stretch then sit on the edge of one of the flowerbeds.

"Good until someone decided to wake the entire neighborhood with his singing." I smile trying not to think of the night before.

"Such a fake smile, what happened?"

I just shrug hoping he would just let it go.

"I know you better than that. Did Garett hurt you?"

I shake my head no.

"Please tell me, you look like you've hardly slept and I can tell that you probably spent the entire night crying your eyes out."

"Sean please, Garett didn't hurt me. It was him that was in pain."

"So he had to keep everyone awake with his singing? Even the dogs were howling? Was he drinking?"

I nod my head in response.

"Figures. Once he starts he can't stop. I don't know why he does it if he knows he has a problem."

I turn to look back at the house as Garett comes out the sliding glass door. He picks up an aluminum bat from the ground and begins to hit rocks over the fence.

"Let's go inside. I'll make you something to eat." Sean says as my stomach growls. I follow him back into the house. I turn to look once more at Garett who is sitting in the spot I recently vacated. He stares down at his feet as he digs holes in the ground with the bat.

I slide the door shut closing out the pain I could hear with each thumping sound the bat made as he hit the soft earth.

Sean comes around the corner carrying a plate with some breakfast burritos on it. This is the second time someone else has made me breakfast in the past three months. I smile at the memory of Garett in the kitchen, frying eggs and bacon for his special eggles. Never in my life had I had a guy, other than my brothers, make me breakfast. I waited for him to cook mine then finish his. We sat at the table and shared our first cooked breakfast together. It's funny how things slowly began to change. Maybe these changes were for the better. Ashley was refusing to talk to Garett. Yeah he was hurt about it right now. Hopefully he'll be able to heal and things will go back to normal. I guess all I can do is sit back and have patients as time works its magic on his wounds.

CHAPTER 10

I went to Nathan's room hoping to find Garett sober. I sit on the bed behind him as he moves his mouse across the screen of his homepage.

"Feeling better" I ask a little snidely.

He turns his chair to face me. "I'm sorry." he says with an ashamed look on his face. "I had a bit too much last night, it won't happen again."

"I hope not. You're forgiven on one condition, don't make me go to bed alone again. I don't mean to sound like I'm nagging or being clingy, its just that I miss hanging out and talking."

He agrees, stands, and then kisses me apologetically. I put my arms between us, laying my hands on his chest. I look at the computer screen and am happy to see he isn't playing the game, but checking his email. I smile as I notice my picture first on his "Friends Page".

"John and Ashley are coming over."

He takes a deep breath and tries to smile. He pulls at a little key on my necklace. This small silver symbol, with the words *key to my heart* sketched across it, was given to me days ago by Garett. He takes my hands in his, leading me to the futon. I sit and let him sit in front of me, leaning against my chest for support.

All of a sudden the chain around my neck breaks. I pull it away from my warm skin, holding it up examining it. Garett tries to fix it as well, "Mom might have an extra chain or something. I'll ask her later." I put it away, feeling strange without its cool metal around my neck. I look at the necklace around his neck and smile as the light catches on the pink stone of his new ring.

"Can I ask you one more favor?" I ask as I sit down with him again.

"If it's reasonable," He smiles playfully.

"No more stumbling to bed. I don't care if you drink; I just don't want to carry you to bed again." He agrees then turns the TV on. Exhausted and glad to have reached a compromise, I curl up and peacefully fall asleep.

I awake to the sound of the front door opening as John and Ashley step in.

"Hey lazies, how's it going?"

I get up and go to brush my teeth, leaving Garett to visit with his cousin. Once the party gets going, John and Ashley decide they are going to be staying the night again. This doesn't sit too well with Garett He begins drinking heavily. After his sixth beer I reminded him of his promise.

"Just one more please?" He gives me his puppy eyes.

"One and then you're done?"

He nods his head, reluctantly I give in. He kisses me then goes to the kitchen, bringing back two beers, one for him and one for me.

"I'm going to geek it up." he begins to walk away. I grab his hand, keeping him from leaving.

"You promised me you wouldn't." he removes his hand from mine and looks me in the eyes.

"No I said I wouldn't make you go to bed alone anymore, besides its still early and I didn't play at all today." He had a good point; I never said he couldn't play it. I really didn't want him to leave me out here alone again. I look at the clock, 10:11. For many people this was the normal hour of going to bed. Since we didn't usually go to bed until one or two in the morning, it was still pretty early.

I give him a serious look, grabbing both of his hands in mine. "Please don't. You can go one day without playing."

He hugs me and kisses my forehead. "I'm going."

"I guess you'll be sleeping on the couch then, I don't want to go to sleep, only to have you come in and wake me up."

"Well I guess I am then."

My mood immediately turns sour as I watch him cross the room, entering Nathan's, closing the door behind him.

"Where is he going to sleep?" Melinda asks, standing next to me. "Are you really going to make him sleep on the couch?"

I shake my head yes.

"Good, if he can't go one day without being on that computer, he doesn't need to be bothering you. If you're going to bed alone you might as well spend the entire night alone.

After a few hours, I go to get ready for bed. I get some pajamas from Nathan's room, not even bothering to speak to Garett. I change in the bathroom then go back in the room to put my dirty clothes away. He smiles at me and I smile falsely back.

"Do I still have to sleep on the couch?"

I think about it for a moment then sigh. That's up to you. I'm going to bed now, if I'm sleeping when you come in, don't even bother waking me up."

"I'll be in there soon."

He looks at me quite seriously. Maybe I'm being childish about all this. Maybe I'm taking his promises to close to heart. He did keep his promise to me and spent the entire day with me, we even watched the sunset for the first time in a while. Then again he was breaking a promise by making me go to bed on my own again. Torn between being mad at him and myself, I leave the room, hurry down the hall, and enter Adam's room. I lean against the closed door for support. I decide to call Brenton for some advice. I tell him about the whole Ashley situation and the drinking episode from last night.

"I don't know what to tell you Michelle. Honestly I just want you to come home. I can't really do much as long as you are two whole states away. He doesn't deserve you; you don't deserve that kind of treatment."

"I can't leave Brenton, for so many reasons. I can't tell you all of them but I can tell you I definitely can't leave, not now."

"Do you love him?" I could hear the pain in his voice as he asks this question.

"With all my heart, that's another reason it's so hard for me. I'm so confused; I don't know what to do."

"Michelle, can I tell you something?"

"You know you can tell me anything."

"Don't get mad."

I agree and wait patiently as he musters up some courage.

"When I found out you left, I was crushed. That last time saw you, when we all got together at the lodge, I felt something. I don't know how to explain it, I just had this feeling it was the last time I was going to get to see you. When I asked if you were going away and you said for a little while, I didn't know you were moving two states away. You didn't even tell me goodbye. That night I realized, watching you and Garett dance together, I was jealous. I realized I still have feelings for you. Hearing the pain in your voice when you talk about everything that's going on over there breaks my heart. I wish there was something I could do to help. It seems a bit impossible as long as you're two states away. You need to be here with your friends and family.

I stubbornly protest and tell him that this family needs me as well. I tell him nothing could ever happen between us, and remind him he has a fiancé he loves greatly and I still love Garett. I couldn't tell him that I feared what would happen if I went home, he didn't need to know about my fear until it was confirmed. After realizing I'm not coming home anytime soon, he gives up and says goodbye. He tells me if I change my mind or need someone to talk to some more, he is just a phone call or text away.

Talking to Brenton leaves me feeling homesick. I think of all the people I left behind and what I would lose if I left. I begin crying, feeling lonely and homesick.

Once my tears subside, I decide to get a drink. I go to the kitchen, grab a cup and fill it to the top with water. I down the water greedily then leave the cup in the sink.

I walk back to the room pausing at Nathan's door, looking in, seeing Garett staring at his MySpace homepage. Before he notices me I return back to bed. Only an hour later Garett comes to bed.

"You still awake?" He asks as I lay silently in his side of the bed. He climbs over me lying next to the wall.

"Depends on what you want."

"Just to talk."

"Then I'm awake."

"I heard you crying earlier." I close my eyes embarrassed. I thought I was being quiet.

"Mom says you come in here and cry sometimes."

"Not for reasons you think, and not all the time."

"Then why?"

I couldn't tell him the real reason, not yet I didn't want him to hate me and push me away. I didn't think he was like a lot of other guys but still I didn't know how he would respond to the news that he could be a father.

"I just got done talking to Brenton. He was telling me how everyone misses me and wants me to come back. I told him that I was just getting over being homesick and I'm staying here."

"If you weren't homesick anymore you wouldn't always be crying. You make me guilty all the time." He stands up, "I think we should see other people." He exit's the room leaving me in shock.

See other people? I know things aren't perfect between us but all couples have their problems, don't they? I'm sure we can work things out. I'm hurt but still hopeful when he comes back into the room five minutes later.

"Michelle?" I ignore him hoping he would think I fell asleep. I wasn't sure how drunk he was and wanted to wait to discuss this when he's sober.

He climbs back in bed.

"I know you're still awake so just hear me out. I got into this relationship with you knowing full and well what I was getting myself into. What I didn't know is that I'm still not over Ashley or Mina."

"What do Mina and Ashley have to do with us?" I ask forgetting I was pretending to be asleep.

"Mina was my first love; I didn't think I could ever truly get over her. As for Ashley, I told you before we were even together that I was waiting for her."

"If you really wanted to be with her then why did you get involved with me for a second time?"

"I saw your face that night at church. I could tell you were hurting really bad. At first I figured you would get over it but then I realized after your texts that you really did care."

"Your mom told me, before I came you were always praying for someone who would truly care and love you. Well I'm here and you're just going to throw that away?"

"Look I didn't ask to be in a relationship right now. I'm just not ready."

"I didn't ask either, People don't generally stand on the side of the streets screaming *I'm ready for a relationship, come on somebody come be with me.* That's not how it works. I didn't ask for this relationship either, it just happened."

Apparently he wasn't too happy with these words. He punches the cement wall then leaves the room angrily again. I just continue laying there in silence trying not to cry.

Another five minutes pass and Garett comes back. This time he lays there in silence for a few minutes.

"Look, I know you're confused right now, emotionally. You don't want to be in a relationship right now. But you need to know, I still love you. I will always be waiting for you. I never lied; you will always be my first and my last, at least until I'm married. It comes with too many emotional attachments."

Garett sighs, removes his necklace, and pulls the ring off of it. He puts the ring on my pillow.

"What are you doing?" I asks picking it up.

"Giving it back to you. I don't want it."

I try handing it back to him. "It's kind of too late for that. It was yours the moment I gave you my Virginity."

"I will always treasure that, but you shouldn't put too much of that value into a stupid ring."

"It's not just a stupid ring."

"Take it back then. How much did you spend on it? It's probably worth a lot. I don't want it."

"I paid eighty five for it but the money doesn't matter to me. It symbolizes my promise to God, everyone, and myself."

"I'm sorry I was the one who made you break your promise."

"Don't!" I snap at him. "Don't ever say you're sorry for it. Even if you don't want me anymore, I do not regret sleeping with you." I put the ring on his pillow. "It's yours, keep it, pawn it, do whatever you want with it. It's yours."

"I don't want it."

"Neither do I."

He gets angry and throws it across the room.

"I guess it's going to stay there."

"I guess so," He says irritated.

Silence falls between us for a few minutes. I turn over to face the door. If I'm going to be sleeping on the edge, I'm at least keeping my eyes on the exit.

"I don't care what you say; I'll still be here when you change your mind."

"I wish you wouldn't "

I close my eyes and whisper, "My offer still stands." With that I fall into a dreamless sleep.

CHAPTER 11

Living with Garett even after the breakup, made it seem like we were still together. The next two days go by pretty strained but by the third day, things were pretty much back to normal. The only thing not in the ordinary is Garett avoids as much physical contact as possible.

Melinda and Brian ask that Garett and I drive Sean back to the town we picked him up in. I didn't mind, the two and a half hour drive there and back would give us time to talk. His family didn't know we weren't together; we were still sleeping in the same room because of the lack of sleeping arrangements. We we're sharing a bed but both have our own separate blankets. The night after the breakup I asked him why he didn't want to be with me.

"I don't need someone telling me what I can and can't do all the time. I want to drink whatever I want, play whatever I want. I'm nineteen, an adult, I shouldn't have a curfew. I don't want to go to bed when someone else decides they're tired. I don't want the responsibility of keeping someone else happy when I have a hard time doing so for myself."

This breaks my heart; I didn't know he considered me to be a responsibility. I let   know about my feelings about my being a burden on him.

"I didn't mean it like that. I just mean that I don't want to be the one who is always making you cry."

I reminded him that it was people from back in Idaho making me cry, not him.

"It doesn't matter; you make me feel guilty for taking you away from your family."

"Do you want me to go back? I really don't want to."

"No. I don't think I could stand it if you went back. It will be a lot easier for me if you stay here. We could always be friends, and stay in touch."

"I'll stay then, it won't be easy for me, but I'll stay."

I reminded him then, and this morning that my offer still stands. I don't care how long it takes or where we end up. I will always be waiting for him to change his mind.

The entire car ride was silent except for Sean telling funny stories. I know he could tell something was wrong between me and Garett. It wasn't until we got out of the car to go find his dad that he asked me about it.

"Did something happen? You and Garett haven't said a word to each other since you guys got up."

I shrug my shoulders trying not to let him see my pain.

"Did you guys get into a fight?" I nod my head holding back the tears.

"We're not together anymore." Sean hugs me and whispers, "I'm sorry. He's stupid, he doesn't know what he's giving up, obviously, otherwise he would never have left you."

The three of us head into the hardware store.

"It would help if I knew what I was looking for." I say following the boys.

"Just look for a silver haired troll."

I thought maybe he was just kidding but soon found out this wasn't the case.

We turn down an aisle and come face to face with a man about five three. This gray haired man extended his hand to me as we're introduced. He shakes it grasping my hand tightly. I grimace in pain, smiling as a cover up. Sean hugs me. "I'll see you soon; I'll be back for spring break in a couple of weeks." He hugs Garett, patting him on the back.

As the two of us exit the store in silence, I mention to Garett how aggressive Sean's dad was. Just by a simple handshake I could tell I didn't like him. This opened up a whole new topic to discuss.

He told me about the time his mom was with him. Tony, was his name, abuse was his game. He would beat Melinda up and abuse her emotionally as well.

"That's why we were living in Hawaii. He wanted to get us away from all our friends and family so we wouldn't have any help." He told me about how eventually they got away from him. Tony had someone video taped Melinda fighting back, they made it look like she was the one that was abusive.

Melinda ended up n jail for domestic violence and the boys ended up in a foster home. I didn't know why he was sharing such private information with me. He told me that even though we weren't together he still loves me and I'm his best friend.

We didn't get back to the house until late that night. I showered then went to the living room. Everyone was getting ready to watch the movie *up*. Melinda passed out some of her brownies. Brian thought it would be cool to watch the cartoon high. He and Melinda ate brownies and smoked while Garett and I stuck with the brownies, eating two or three a piece. Throughout the movie I would turn to watch Garett intently watching the screen. I didn't know if he was really into it or if he was just so lost in thought. This would be a great time to have thought reading capabilities. Once the movie ends I go to bed, forgetting to separate the blankets. Not wanting to disturb me, Garett just crawls in beside me. I turn over to face him.

"How did you like the movie?"

"It seemed a little sad for a Disney movie."

"That's because is Pixar not Disney."

"Well, Disney or Pixar, it's still supposed to be a kid's movie. The whole movie was basically about the old ladies death. If I were a kid I wouldn't want to watch it."

"It has a happy ending."

"What's that? You grow up, get old, lose your closest companion, and then have to live alone again. Grumpy and lonely?"

"I guess you can look at it that way or you can look at it as an adventure."

"An adventure that's only fun if you get to share it with someone special."

He has a good point; I wouldn't want to grow old, going through it on my own.

"Everyone gets the opportunity to share it with someone special."

"Not me."

"What do you mean?" Hello I'm lying right here you can

make the choice.

"I'll be on the ship, alone. I already told you, I'm not going to be with anyone else."

"You know you don't have to be alone; I still love you, I'll wait for you."

He sighs and rubs his face with his fingertips.

"You're never going to give up are you?"

"Nope, I'm promising you right now, you don't have to take the adventure alone."

Silence settles in, he sighs loudly.

"What?"

"Nothing, it's a guy thing."

Of course he would be thinking about sex. I wasn't going to give in tough, unless I had some sort of commitment; no matter how much I wanted to.

He sighs again.

"Don't even think about it."

"Why not? You still love me don't you?"

"Yes but it takes more than that."

"I love you too and you're still my best friend."

Oh no he didn't, there is no way he is pulling the whole friends with benefits card on me.

"I don't think so." I sound disgusted.

"Why not? Friends do it all the time."

"Because it's weird and I value sex. It's not just an action people do; it comes with emotions. I have to have some kind of commitment."

I continue staring at him as he stares back. He puts his hand to my face and brushes my hair back.

"Garett, no matter how badly I want to, I can't without knowing we are together."

"But we are together, why do titles matter so much?"

I had to think about this for a minute. I am utterly confused now, are we or are we not together?

"I guess titles aren't that big of a deal."

Being called his girlfriend let everyone know we were together. If they didn't know about the breakup, they would still think we were together. Not much has changed the only exception being, he doesn't kiss me anymore. What I wouldn't give to have his soft lips on mine again.

As if he could read my thoughts, he leans over and kisses me passionately. For the first time in a few days I felt my body come alive. My heart breaks with joy as my tongue explores the familiar taste of his mouth. Slowly he lowers his hands, skimming his fingers down my body. He stops at the bottom of my t shirt, places his cold hands underneath the thin fabric, then slowly runs his hands up my side, my breasts, my neck, then finally lifts me, pulling my shirt over my head. He runs his hand down my spine, unhooks my bra, and then returns to kissing me.

"I've missed you." I whisper to him, a tear escaping the corner of my eye. He smiles as tears run down his face.

"I missed you too."

He kisses me again, this time as if he would die without my lips. Again the pain was excruciating but soon turned to pleasure. For the first time, I finished at the same time as him, leaving my muscles screaming in ecstasy. I lay there in his strong embrace, thoughts racing through my mind. He kisses my forehead.

"I wonder if it hurts, getting old I mean." I say playing with his hand. "Getting wrinkles and gray hair is probably the easiest part. The aches and pains from the years of wear and tear are probably the worst; I bet the memories make it all worthwhile."

"Not if you live with a lot of regrets and painful memories. Not if you end up alone."

I roll my eyes and give up.

"Would you rather live forever?"

"No."

"Me neither, I would hate it; life would get pretty boring."

I hope when it's my turn to go someone will either shoot me, or I get abducted."

"Yeah because that's the way to go. I'm not afraid of death. I'm afraid of the pain, in case you haven't noticed; I'm a crybaby when it comes to pain."

How did we get on such a morbid topic anyway? We lay in silence. All of a sudden Garett turns his head to look at me then turns away abruptly, turns to look at me again then turns away again.

"Kevin!" I say laughing, putting my hand up to stop him from doing it anymore.

"Kevin?"

"Yeah, when you do that, you remind me of the bird on the movie, Kevin." We both laugh at our new inside joke as he does it some more.

"Goodnight… I love you, sweet dreams." I say turning so that I'm facing the door. He continues holding me.

"Goodnight, I love you, sweet dreams." He says kissing the back of my head.

I loved this Garett; this was the old Garett, the one that wasn't drunk, the one that I fell in love with. I don't know how long this will last but I'm going to take all that I can get. In this moment, I am Garett's girlfriend again, even without the title. We are together, sober, and happy.

"Mommy, Where's daddy, I can't find daddy. Why did he leave us? Does he not love us anymore?" The little girl in my dream smiles at me as I pull Garett from out behind a tree. "Daddy's here. He's back sweetie."

Garett picks up the little girl, kissing her and tossing her in the air.

"Why did you go away daddy? Didn't you want us anymore?" He smiles kissing away her tears. I stand back and watch as he pushes her on an old wooden swing set. For some reason I had a feeling he wasn't staying long. He was only here for a moment then he was going to disappear again. How was I ever going to tell this little girl? She seemed happy now that I've accepted her as my daughter. I don't think I can live with myself if I had to be the one to tell her that Garett was leaving again.

The two of them smile and wave, then begin playing tag. Running in and out from between all the trees. I join in and enjoy the moment while it lasts.

As the sun comes streaming through the window I open

my eyes. I feel Garett's arm tucked gently around my waist and continue laying there thinking about my dream. It's only a matter of time before I have to tell him of my dreams. They scared me at first; they had me thinking I was pregnant. I'll just have to wait another week at least until I tell Garett. I don't want there to be a lot of stress put on him or anyone else, at least until I'm absolutely sure. I'll just play it out and act like everything is normal.

I feel Garett move, and turn over to face him. I can't help smiling at his placid expression. His eyes sparkle as he smiles back.

"Good morning." He says rubbing something from my eye with his gentle finger.

"My favorite time of day."

"Whys that?"

I stretch and pull the blankets over me, locking in the warmth.

"It's the start of a new day; a fresh start, a clean slate."

He smiles and lies with me a moment longer. After he gets up he picks up the extra blanket, spreading it out over me.

"Well I'm glad someone enjoys the mornings." He puts on his clothes then leaves the room, leaving me to think of our strange night.

I still have no idea what our relationship status is. He says he doesn't want the titles. Does that mean we are together? After last night I would think so, I'm going to keep believing that until he gives me reason to believe otherwise.

CHAPTER 12

After I finally drag my comfortable butt out of bed, I spend the day how I usually spend it, watching Garett play his game. In the evening he began drinking again. I couldn't really say anything to him about how I like it much better when he's sober. When he drinks he becomes a whole other person. I don't want to say he's mean, I can't really explain it. When he's drunk is when I get hurt the most. That night I text Brenton and tell him how badly I want to go back to Idaho, but also tell him the reasons I want to stay.

Maybe Garett will change. Last night he told me we were together without titles. I'm sure I can handle that until he's ready.

His reply: *You just sent me a long text with more negatives than positives; do you want to come back or not? If you truly want to stay then there's not much I can do. All I can say is good luck.*

I put my phone on the nightstand and wait for Garett to come in. I lay there for hours before finally going to check on him at midnight. I go down the hall, surprised to find Nathan's room void of him. I didn't want to invade his privacy, but after the other night's fiasco, I couldn't help but worry. I walk out into the dark living room, finding it empty of everyone except the dogs curled up in front of the lit fireplace. As I begin to leave the living room, I hear Garett's voice coming from the sliding glass door. He comes inside talking on the phone. I didn't want him to think I was eavesdropping, but his hushed tone made me curious so I stopped to listen for a minute. Something in the way he was talking made me think it wasn't his cousin he was talking to. Could it be Ashley?

He finally came stumbling in a few hours later. Great here we go again.

He tries to climb into bed but hits his shins on the frame. He falls forward ungracefully. I sit up and glare at his still body. If he thinks I'm going to take pity on him again for being drunk, He's nuts. "Are you going to stay like that or are you going to come up here?" I listen and hear his soft sobs. "Garett... Are you going to be okay?" All is silent except for the sound of his soft crying. "Garett, I can't help you if you don't talk to me." He stops crying, after a few minutes of silence he says he has to pee.

"You should have thought about that before you got so drunk you can't even stand." I can't let him just lie here and pee the bed. But how can I help him? He only wants help physically. If I help him that way what would it lead to? I give in, telling myself it's because I don't want to wake up in a puddle of his urine.

I stand up and pull him to his feet. I put his arm around my neck and he leans all his weight on me as we shuffle off to the bathroom. I hope he knows I'm done. Yeah I'll keep my promise and wait for him. If it was Ashley he was talking to, he has made it pretty clear that we are not together as I thought we were. Last night would be the last night having sex with him until I was sure we were together. There was no way I was going to play the friends with benefits game.

I get him into the bathroom where he convinces me he can hold himself up with the sink. I wait outside the door, waiting to help him back to bed.

Once I drag his butt through the door I feel all his weight press on me. "Come on Garett, we're almost there." Unable to move any further, he lays his head on my shoulder and drapes his body across me.

I'm not going to feel sorry for him, not this time. Sure I'll help him to bed, I still care. If he wants to drink himself to death, there's not really much I can do. I've already talked to him about it, what more can I do but talk?

"I'm sorry." He says as he begins to cry. I try my hardest to keep him from seeing the pain he is inflicting on me. This fuels some kind of anger in me, motivating me to drag him the rest of the way to the bed.

"Please don't hate me."

"I don't hate you Garett, I m mad that you broke your promises, but I don't hate you. I could never."

"I'm sorry." He whispers again, still crying.

I really can't hate him, no matter what he chooses to do. Hating him would be like hating myself. Yeah I'm completely disappointed with him whenever he drinks himself to this. I hate how he makes me feel sorry for him when he's dumb enough to make such bad choices. I hate how he makes me feel so confused, he knows what he wants, it would be nice if he would just clue me in already. One minute everything is fine and dandy, the next he is drunk and depressed.

"I'm sorry too." I say as he puts his arm around me. I remove it from around my waist, close my eyes and fall asleep.

Not more than twenty minutes later I hear a noise. I open my eyes to find a man sitting on the nightstand. I'm terrified, frozen stiff. All I can do is breath. That in itself is hard because of the putrid smell coming off the raggedy old man. He sits there staring at me. Obviously he isn't here to hurt me otherwise he would have done so by now. I stay silent, watching him for about another minute. He looks to be homeless in his dirty torn clothes. The only good thing on his body that I can see, is his tan leather jacket,

Wh...What do you want?" I ask him quietly, my voice quivering.

He simply begins laughing then says "Go home." After repeating himself several times, I turn to see if Garett is seeing any of this. To my amazement he is still asleep. Surely the loudness of the man's laugh would have woken him by now.

I shake Garett's body and call out to him. All of a sudden the laughing stops and Garett opens his eyes sleepily.

"What is it? He asks a little worry coating his voice.

"The man behind me, how did he get in here?"

Garett pokes his head up lazily. "What are you talking about, there's no one else in the room."

I turn around to find the room empty. "He was right there. I saw him."

"How many brownies did you have?"

I give him a dirty look. "Two. It wasn't a hallucination, he was sitting right there laughing."

He gives me a skeptical look.

"I'm not crazy."

He insisted that it was just a hallucination. I decided not to argue with him. I lay my head back on the pillow, keeping a look out for anymore strange men in the room. Before I know it I'm fast asleep.

The entire next day All I could think about was the man telling me to go home. Maybe it was my subconscious letting me know that I really wanted to go home. I was hoping last night was all, as Garett said, a hallucination. That night we went to bed, after a while I heard a noise again. This time I was less afraid and more relieved to see this strange man sitting on the night stand again. This time he had my phone in his hand, reading a text message. He laughs again and tells me to go home. He repeats himself over and over again until I wake Garett up.

"How much have you had to drink?"

"None. I'm not crazy; I'm telling you he was right there."

He puts his hand on mine, trying to comfort me. "We'll go sleep somewhere else if you're worried."

"No, its fine for tonight." I could have been dreaming I suppose. "Obviously he wasn't here to hurt me."

We discuss other things, he tells me some more stories from his past, keeping my mind busy until I fall asleep.

The next morning I open my eyes to see Garett already awake, staring at me. We lay there and discuss our plans for the day. Once he leaves I decide to call my cousin Ashley. When I go to reach for my phone, I find it lying open, my message to Brenton lit up on the screen. Chills crawl down my spine as I read the text; it was the one I mentioned all the reasons for me to go back to Idaho. It was the same one the man was reading last night. Could this be a sign?

I told Melinda of the man and told her how he randomly disappeared. She told me that there was a woman, a ghost, who pretty much lived in Adam's room.

"Maybe it's her husband."

I told her I really didn't want to sleep on there anymore. She tells me she will move Nathan out to the living room and Garett and I could have his room.

"You'll have to hang in therefore a couple of night while we get everything situated."

"I don't want to put anyone out of there room." I guess I can stay with the ghost, or whatever he was. I'd rather not make anyone uncomfortable just because I'm afraid of things that go bump in the night.

"Adam's going to be home soon anyway. He'll want his room back and I'm sure you and Garett aren't going to want to do anything in the living room again."

I could feel my cheeks turn bright red.

"Oh I forgot; you guys wouldn't be doing anything anyway."

Melinda and Brian only found out about the breakup yesterday. I went to work with them, on the way home we stopped at Wal-Mart for some gardening supplies and tampons. Brian grabbed a box of condoms and said he would buy them for Garett and me.

"I don't think we'll be using them anytime soon." I look away feeling uncomfortable, having to tell his parents about everything.

Melinda puts her arm around my shoulders. "You can still have sex that time of the month. Just lay a towel down."

Ewww, that's the most disturbing thing I have ever heard.

"That's not the problem." I take a deep breath, bracing myself for the pain. "We aren't together anymore. He broke up with me the other night."

She just looks at me, "You're still sleeping together."

"Yes but not having sex. Most of the time we have our own blankets."

"I'm sure you guys will get back together. What are you guys fighting about anyway?"

I explain the whole Ashley situation and Garett's drinking episode.

"He'll come around I'm sure. He just has an obsession for her. When he figures out that she only wants a daddy for her baby and she doesn't really love him like you do, he'll snap out of it. If he wants to be with you without the titles, he can pretend you are just friends, everyone else knows you are his girlfriend. He's just trying to make Ashley happy. I don't know why he is so obsessed, he needs to wake up and see he has all that he needs right here."

Brian tosses the box into the basket. I'm not giving them to Garett. I hid them in the green tote with my clothes. He can have them when I know for sure what he wants.

Once again I end up going to bed alone. I only went because I was hoping Garett would come in and talk to me. Obviously I would have to go to him. I go to Nathan's room, sit quietly on the bed behind Garett's chair. I watch as he plays his game and listen to the music that's playing. I see the remnants of his drinking as he turns the game off and just stares at his MySpace profile, listening to the music. He turns slightly in his chair, looking back at me. His eyes sparkle with torment. I wanted so badly to get up and run as far away as possible. I was tired of loving him with all my heart when obviously he didn't feel the same way. I know he is talking to Ashley again. She was now first on his friends list, leaving me to take second. Sometimes I would watch him stare at the pictures, not knowing if it was hers or mine that she was staring at. It takes a lot of energy to love someone that loved another.

I just don't understand how he can look at me with the guilt and passion he is showing me now. He reaches his hand out to me. Does he expect me to take it? If I take the leap I won't be able to turn back. Will I hit the ground or will he catch me? He reaches his hand out further, giving me a look of desperation. I close my eyes and ignoring my conscious, slide to the edge of the bed and take his hand in mine. He entwines his fingers around mine, continuing to give me that sad look.

"Garett…" He closes his eyes taking a deep breath "I can't keep pretending everything is okay. I can't keep doing this to myself."

He rolls the chair back and pulls me to my knees so that

I'm at his eye level. Sitting between his knees I rest my arms in his lap.

The look of pain in his eyes scares me. What could possibly be wrong? He has what he wants what more could he ask for?

"Garett, tell me what you want. I'm not a mind reader and to be honest you keep changing every other night, I really don't know what to do to make you happy" I say almost in tears.

He puts his hands on my arms. "I just need time to figure things out. If you can have patience, we'll work things out, I promise."

"Work things out how? As in we'll be together?"

His eyes, glassy with tears, study my hopeful gaze.

"Just promise me you'll be patient." I smile and nod.

Promise me that in the meantime, if someone else comes along that you find you really like, and you think you can be happy with him; Promise me you'll go with him. You won't continue waiting, It could be my brother for all I care just please do it to be happy. Promise me that you won't turn him down just because you are waiting for me."

What the heck is he trying to say? Is there or is there not a possibility of us getting together again officially?

"I can't promise that. That would mean I have to break my other promise, I'm not going to do it."

"Please, Michelle do it for me. You deserve to be happy even if I'm not."

"No. I'm not going to promise you that, I can't, I don't think I could ever be happy with someone else."

"That's why you have to try. Please for me. If you really love me like you say you do, you'll promise me."

That's not fair, now I have to. If he's trying to hurt me even more, congratulations, it's working."

"Fine. I promise, but don't expect me to be happy about it though. One way or another I'll be breaking a promise." He pulls me even closer and kisses me. My confused mind goes blank and I forget that I'm supposed to be mad at him.

The song changes from the slow one to a fast one by

Biggie Smalls. He stands up, pushing his chair away and begins dancing. He does a dance, copying his character from his game. I laugh at his W.O.W. dance and he pulls me to my feet to dance with him. I've danced to faster songs before, usually by myself or in a big group of girls, never one on one with a guy so it was a little awkward. I'm sure if someone was watching they would die of laughter.

When the song ends he shuts down his computer and leads me to bed. This was the second time I stupidly slept with him thinking we were together again. Why was it so easy for him to make me forget? With a simple kiss he could make me forget every ounce of pain and make me believe I was his only love.

Just like the time before, the next morning he was back to pretending I wasn't there. I walked by his computer, noting his mood status. *What a crazy night.* I was sorry to say that I agree with this. It was disappointing that he thought so, but I guess I couldn't complain. It takes two to tango. I roll my eyes at this expression my mother would always use. I couldn't believe it; she was two states away and could still get inside my head with her stupid sayings. Sometimes I wish I can talk to her about what's going on over here. Of course she definitely wouldn't approve and would try to lecture me. I wish I had a friend to talk to that wouldn't have a biased opinion.

Suddenly my phone rings. I look at the caller ID, *Ashley.* It's funny how she always calls just when I need her too, or when I'm just thinking about her. If we didn't look so different I would think we were twins separated at birth.

"How's it going with you and Garett?"

She already knew about all the drama going on. She called the other day while Garett was buried in his computer.

"He's talking to Ashley again. He tries to hide it but I'm not stupid. His mom said she was going to take her phone away from him and not let him use it anymore but he always ends up with it anyway. I don't know if I can stay here and continue getting hurt day in and day out."

"Why don't you come home then? You could come back

and everything will go back to how it was before." I could hear the tears in her voice.

I hate hearing the pain every time I talk to her. She is my best friend in the whole world; can I really give her up for a guy who doesn't even know if he loves me anymore? What am I thinking? Of course I couldn't, that's why I talk to her almost every day, listening to her cry.

"I can't come home Ashley. I have to stay." She still doesn't know I suspect I'm pregnant. I want so badly to tell her right now, just so I could have someone to help me carry this secret. I don't tell her though, I can't risk anyone else finding out before Garett. I will tell him eventually. As selfish as it sounds, I can't find out on my own, if I take a test and it's positive, I'll have to explain to him that I've been keeping this from him as well as the fact that whether he wants me or not he is the father of my child. I'm terrified to find out what his reaction will be like; I've decided to wait at least two weeks after my missed period. It seems to get harder and harder every day to keep a smile and hold my thoughts in. There are two things that I fear the most if the test come out positive. I fear Garett won't want to step up and take responsibility. I don't want my child to grow up without a father as I had to. The only other thing I fear is that He would think I made this happen just so he would stay with me. This is not the kind of girl I am. I could deal with him being with someone else as long as he would be a proud parent and help me take care of our child.

"You still there?" I hear Ashley's voice coming through to me.

"Yeah sorry. I was thinking."

"Michelle, please come home. Not just for me, your brothers miss you too."

A tear slides down my cheek and I swipe it away. I hate thinking about home. I miss it too much and think about going back to often that I normally try to block my family from my mind.

"I'll come and visit soon, I promise. When I do we'll go see a movie at the drive in."

I know this would cheer her up. Going to the movies was our thing we did together. If it wasn't closed for the winter we would go to the local drive in. If it was too cold or we just didn't have the money, we would stay home and watch movies all night.

We both begin to cry as we reminisce all the good times we've had.

"I have to go, Grandma needs to use the phone, call me tomorrow."

I agree and hang up feeling empty and lonely. I go back to Nathan's room where Brian and Melinda are removing his broken bed and cleaning out the room for me and Garett. I toss all my stuff in the tote and clean up all the toys. Once everything is cleaned and ready, I decide to go to bed. I lay under the blankets and watch Garett type as he listens to music. I can't see the words or anything without my glasses but I can make out Ashley's picture at the top of the message. I turn to face the wall hoping he doesn't turn around and see me crying.

"You want the light off?" He asks without turning around.

"Its fine, I can sleep with it on." Politely he leans over and snaps the switch off. Twenty minutes later he shuts the computer down and slides into bed.

"Michelle…"

"What?" I whisper, trying to keep my voice from quivering.

"Do you think I've changed?"

I didn't want to answer this question. I didn't want to hurt him with the truth. He has change in so many ways; Most of them were for the worst. The whole drinking thing and Ashley obsession to name a few.

"I think you have changed. Not all for the good but you do have some qualities that make you better."

He quietly thinks this over.

"Why?"

"Just wondering."

"Garett?"

"Hmm?"

"Have I changed?"

He hesitates for a minute.

"Honestly, you seem less happy, more depressed. It makes me feel guilty."

No kidding, gee I wonder why. Sitting here all day being completely ignored and then used would make a person unhappy. To top it off, keeping a huge secret and fearing the reaction once it comes out, yep I'd say that would do the trick. I don't confide in him but simply say, "Oh… I'm sorry; I'll try to be happier."

"See that's the problem right there, you shouldn't have to try. You should just get to be happy. That's what makes me feel so guilty. You were such a happy person when we first got here. Now you have to pretend all the time just so you don't make me feel bad."

This makes me feel guilty. "That's not true, I am happy. Maybe not as much as I used to be. Everyone is entitled to be sad or angry sometimes. No one can be happy twenty four seven. You need to get a grip on reality and stop feeling guilty."

It would help if you would make up your mind and choose who you really want to be with.

We got into a fight one night because I pointed out the fact that I'm right here not two inches from him, Ashley is all the way in Texas. I was here trying to get him to love me as much as I love him. She was over there taking care of her baby, trying to get over her baby's daddy. Why couldn't he see what he already has? Why am I not good enough for him? I would jump through hoops to do anything he asks me. Love doesn't come around very often. Sure you can love someone but you can't truly love just anyone. I'm not talking about the hugs and kisses I love you. I'm talking about; I love you enough that if you were dying I would take your place in a heartbeat without even thinking about the consequences. The kind of love where you steel all the pain from them and put it all on yourself just so they don't have to feel it. The kind of love where you take them home and promise that they are safe and nothing bad can ever happen to them. I don't believe that kind of love ever goes away. I know that it will always be there in my heart, nagging and reminding me of everything that we had, and still can have if only he would make up his mind.

I don't think it will ever truly leave his heart either. Even if we grow old without each other, this will be one of those regrets and painful memories he doesn't want to live with.

This is one of the many reasons I promised I would always wait for him. Number one, I don't think I could ever get over him. Even after all the pain he has caused me, I still love him with all my heart. I would gladly take all his pain, he only has to say the words and I would gladly make him the happiest man on earth. The second reason I promised, I knew that deep down he loves me with all his heart as well. All the drinking and his obsession with Ashley have him blinded. I can see it when he's sober, so I know it's there somewhere. If only there was some way to get him to stop drinking. I was talking to Brian about it the other night. He said he knows as well as Garett that he has a problem. With Garett it's never just one glass of wine or one beer, its drink until you're ready to pass out. That's when I tried to limit Garett's drinking. I was trying to protect him, look where that got me. I wish I could get it through to him that life wasn't all about drinking. I tried talking to him about it but he ended up pushing me away. I can only sit back and watch as he drinks himself into oblivion and then help him put himself together again.

About a week goes by, Garett and I have been sleeping on the same twin size mattress, on the floor of Nathan's room. I would sit and read or text Brenton every day, all day While Garett would play his game, listen to music, and text Ashley.

He would no longer sneak off to talk to her. He would sit there right in front of me and text her. This hurt, as if someone punched a hole in my heart. At least when he would sneak off and talk to her I didn't always know he was talking to her. Now though I would have to watch as he excitedly picked the phone up to text her back all day. Finally I got

tired of it and would spend my days in the living room
with Brian and Melinda.

One morning Melinda invited us to go to the Santa Rosa
mall. We were on speaking terms and I was beginning to deal
with the fact that we were just friends for now, so we were
both looking forward to the trip. Once we got out of the car, I
was a little shocked and surprised when Garett held my hand.
We walked through all of the stores hand in hand, at one
point we even stopped and he wrapped his arms around me,
kissing my forehead.

Maybe I was reading too much into his silence. Maybe I
was patient enough and he was finally coming back to me.
All I know is standing there in his arms, I felt home again.

During the car ride home I fell asleep with my head on
his chest.

We went to bed as if none of the Ashley stuff had
happened. He sweetly made love to me and we laid there
talking. He gets up to open the door leading to outside then
slides back in bed. We lay there listening to the rain fall on
the concrete outside.

"You know, we haven't talked like this since our first
phone conversation." He says playing with my fingers.

"I wonder why that is." I say yawning deeply.

"We never really needed to I guess. When we were first
together we didn't see each other every minute of every day.
Now that we sit together all day we know exactly what goes
on so there's no need to talk about it."

He tickles me, making his alien finger sound.

"I love you" I say as he runs his fingers through my hair.

He looks at me with his passionate eyes, "I love you too."
He lowers his lips to mine and kisses me. I could feel all the
pain and unease between us slowly melt away. I know this is
the perfect time to tell him about my suspected pregnancy.
The moment was so sweet I didn't want to ruin it. Before I
get the chance to say anything, Garett is sleeping, his arm
once again wrapped around me. I tuck my feet under his legs
to keep them warm then slowly drift to sleep.

CHAPTER 13

I wake to the sound of the bedroom door opening. Sean stands at the foot of the bed where he drops all his stuff onto the floor. I sit up making sure the blankets are fully covering my naked body.

"I thought we were coming to get you."

He smiles, "Surprise, my dad dropped me off."

"Sweet, you're early. Can you go out so I can get dressed? I'm going to take a shower too then I'll be out there."

Sean looks at Garett then back at me. I roll my eyes and tell him to go before he wakes his brother.

Once the door is closed I throw on some clothes and head to the bathroom. I race through my shower and grooming process. I toss my dirty clothes and wet towel into the laundry then run to Sean, giving him a great big bear hug.

"Long time no see stranger.' He says trying to loosen my grip so he can breathe.

"How long do you get to stay?" I ask excitedly.

"I'm here for all of spring break."

"Sweet."

"How are you and Garett? I noticed you two were a little cozy in there." He nudges me with his elbow. "I take it you two are back together?"

"To be honest, I'm really not sure. He gives me whiplash, one minute everything is great between us, the next thing you know he's all emo, drunk, and depressed."

"That's the alcohol taking over him. I don't know why everyone lets him drink, they know he has a problem."

We go to the backyard and I bring him up to speed. He tells me everything that went on back home. We discussed music and pass the time making fun of songs that we both hate then go in to play rock band.

Melinda and Brian come home from work around seven and break out the wine. I hesitantly take the glass she was holding out to me. I went easy and only had two glasses while everyone else had a few more. Garett comes out of the room carrying his empty glass. He sets it on the table and places his hands on my shoulders.

"Don't you dare! Don't you even touch her." Melinda yells pointing her finger at him. "You think you can pretend to be her possessive boyfriend out in public and then come here and not want anything to do with her? I don't think so. You don't touch her."

I felt a little relief yet disappointed when he put his hands up in surrender and walked away. Melinda pulled me down the hall to have a little pep talk.

"Don't let him do that to you. If he can't love you at home as he does in public, you don't need him. He sits there and ignores you while he talks to Ashley, until he wants something. You can't let a guy treat you like that. Do you know what that makes him? I'm sorry to say it because he is my son and I love him, but it makes him a bastard. No guy is worth it, especially him. I know he's my son and I love him for that, but I hate it when he treats you like crap. Don't think for a minute that I buy in to your smile and false peppy attitude, I know you're hurting inside and you really don't deserve it. You are and amazing woman that doesn't see how strong and beautiful she really is. If only you could see what everyone else sees."

She often gave me these pep talks, I'm glad though, it shows she cares and it makes me feel better about myself.

I was feeling good and play fighting with Sean when Garett emerged from the room again. He put his hands up and grabbed my fists as I pretended to punch him. We stand there for a minute before he says, "You're not allowed to touch me."

"No you're not allowed to touch me, remember." I didn't mean to make him mad, but he retreated, leaving me standing there with my fists extended. As he walks to the kitchen, probably to get the vodka, I drop my hands and go back to the futon with everyone else. Ten minutes later I have to pee, when I reach the bathroom I hear Garett in there puking his guts out. I decide to use the other bathroom then go back to my place in the living room.

"Where's Garett?" Brian asks, hoping he would play the drums.

"Puking his guts out."

"You're kidding me." his mom yells getting up and standing next to the bathroom door. As soon as Garett comes out she tells him he's cut off.

"why?"

"Because you're always drinking, even when you're throwing up you don't think you've had enough."

After arguing with her for a few minutes he gives up and locks himself in the room again.

"I'm so embarrassed, you have no idea."

I decide it's time for me to go to bed. I didn't want to sit out there and feel any more uncomfortable than I already was.

"Goodnight sis. Love you." Sean whispers, poking his head in through the door, once I'm in bed and settled.

"Goodnight I love you too."

I'm wide awake when Garett opens the back door and comes to bed. It's raining again, only this time it isn't romantic. The staccato of the raindrops hitting the cement accentuated the silence.

"I'm not drunk by the way. I threw up dinner, none of it was alcohol."

I could tell he wasn't drunk, buzzed maybe but not even close to puking drunk. I let him know that I believe him. We stay up talking for a while. I finally fall asleep to the sound of his deep breathing.

CHAPTER 14

Adam comes home; he is nothing what I pictured. Everything I had heard about him described a rugged, tight laced, military man. My first impression of him was that he was a cute cuddly teddy bear. Talking to him and getting to know him taught me that my first impression wasn't far off. He was soft spoken and didn't have anything bad to say about anyone. He wasn't much of a drinker but had a couple of raspberry drinks as everyone else drank the harder stuff. Garett and I were fighting again and Adam asked me about it. Melinda and I brought him up to speed while Brian and I cooked dinner. He already knew about the Texas and Ashley thing, all we told him about was the drinking, computer playing, and Ashley texting obsession. Adam gave me a sorrowful look.

"How could he do this to you?"

"I don't know, you want to know the most hurtful part of all this?" I say slurring a bit. I know I shouldn't have been drinking; I talked to Sean and finally told him my secret. He said that the first couple of weeks a woman can drink without hurting the fetus. I didn't want to risk it, up until now I hadn't had enough to get drunk. I had to keep pretending for at least another week until I would finally tell him.

"The worst part is knowing that he loved me so much at one point. He makes me feel bad for still caring. I don't want to seem clingy or anything but he needs to know that I'm not going to just sit back and let him ignore me until he wants something."

I show Adam the text messages saved on my phone. They were all from Garett, the ones where he's talking about how I'm such a great kisser, the break up because of Ashley, and the ones stating we are officially back together.

"I don't understand him; he's never been like this before."

"It's all the drinking." Brian says stirring the asparagus again.

"Well I say if he wants to be with her so badly, Ill ship his butt to Texas. Let him get his heart broken again, and then find his own way home. He has no right to treat you like this. I just can't believe you stayed this long. If I were you, I would have gotten in my car and headed back to Idaho weeks ago."

I smile at his concern and think about my secret. My stomach does a back flip as guilt rushes over me. What the heck am I doing? Just because I'm mad at Garett, doesn't mean I should be taking it out on my child. I put my hands on my stomach as I whisper a little prayer that God will protect and not punish my baby for my stupidity. I stumble down the hall, feeling horrible.

Melinda comes over and asks what's wrong. I glance at the closed bedroom door where I can just picture Garett excitedly texting Ashley.

"Don't. He's not worth it. I thought we already had this talk. I thought we decided you don't need him and you're going to move on."

I close my eyes and begin to silently cry.

"I can't."

"You can."

"No I can't, I can't because it hurts so much. It feels like he ripped my heart out and shoved it down my throat, now he's sitting back and laughing at my pain. Why does he like her so much more than me? Why am I not good enough?"

She goes to her room and comes back minutes later carrying a bible. I thought she was going to read me some comforting scriptures. Instead she opens the front cover and removes a picture that breaks my heart even more. "Look at her. She's not even pretty. Look at that." She shoves the picture in my face and continues making fun of Ashley's picture.

"She's making a silly face, other than that she's beautiful." I glare at the slender, black haired girl who was the cause of all my pain.

"She is not. Besides that she is nothing but a whore. When Garett went down there she was screwing that Mexican daddy that knocked her up. She didn't want anything to do with Garett until the father up and left her to take care of her child all on her own."We both agreed that she only wanted him so she could have a daddy for her baby. Self consciously I place my arms around my stomach. If only he knew. He's going to find out soon, he might have a child of his own to take care of.

"Adam wants to ship him to Texas."

I say slightly worried. This is something I definitely don't want to happen.

"That sounds like a good Idea to me. He's an adult and wants to make up his own rules. Good luck to him, when you have a baby you have to take care of its needs when it wants, not when you want. I give him less than a month before he's calling for me to come get him or send him money to get home. That's how it usually is, he'll get mad at me and want to leave, usually he ends up going to my mom's but he always ends up calling for a ride or money. I'm not going to do it if he goes to Texas. I won't be the one to bail him out; he can find his own way back."

I don't know, I think he would stay there longer. He told me once; the first time leaving home is the hardest. After the second or third time it becomes a piece of cake. What if he decides he likes it down there?

"Even if he does go, I want you to know you are more than welcome to continue staying here. From now on you are here as my guest not Garett's."

After her little pep talk, we all eat then do our own thing. I decide to go hang out with Sean while Garett sits and plays on the computer again.

We hook Sean's play station three up to the TV in the bedroom. He gets online and we look up music videos. When we decide it's time to settle down, we lie on the bed and watch ghost videos. Garett becomes more interested in the videos than his game and comes to lie in bed next to me.

I take it Ashley is done texting him for the night because the phone remains silently laying on the desk next to the computer. We kick Sean out, deciding it's time for bed.

Garett opens the back door then climbs in under the covers. We tell more ghost stories and laugh at each other for being such scaredy cats. Just as silence settles in, a loud bang comes from the door and echoes throughout the room.

"What the heck was that?" Garett asks as my heart races.

"I have no idea; maybe it was a ghost, or worse, and alien. You should go check it out." I say sarcastically

"No way, If it's an alien it'll abduct me." He says in false terror.

I squint through the darkness and laugh as, Garett's cat jumps onto the screen and climbs up the window.

"It's only the cats you big baby."

He playfully pushes me against the wall. "You were afraid too."

I wait until he is least expecting it then push him, making him roll off the mattress onto the hard floor.

"Maybe we should tome it down a bit on the whole ghost and alien thing. I wouldn't want to have nightmares."

We talk a little longer then fall asleep to the sound of the cats playing outside the door.

"Mommy…Mommy…Mommy…" My little girl holds my hand and runs in circles, spinning me with her excitedly. I pick her up and toss her high in the air. She laughs her sweet laugh and begs me to do it again. I haven't had the heart to tell her that Garett was gone again. This would be so much easier, not only on me, but also on our daughter, if he would just make up his mind already. I don't know how much longer I can keep lying to her just to protect her. She asked me one time where he goes when he is away for so very long. I don't know who I try to convince more, her or myself. I know the truth; I know that he didn't want this family. For some reason he wanted us, but he didn't want the responsibility of a family. He'd much rather spend some time with us and then leave when he's gotten his fill, to be with Ashley.

"Mommy… I want to go home, I want Daddy."

I scoop her up in my arms and bury her head in my chest to keep her from seeing my tears.

CHAPTER 15

I wake up, my cheeks wet with tears, to the sound of my phone vibrating under my pillow. I flip it open and find a text from Brenton.

Did you tell him?

Great, now that he knows, he's not going to stop bugging me about it until I tell him. I close my phone, choosing to ignore him.

"Who is it?" Garett asks, probably hoping it's one of my brothers.

My brother Antony is usually the one that is always texting him. Just the other night, after having sex, my brother was texting me asking me all kinds of questions about it. I tried to get him to change the subject but somehow it ended up changing back. It was the most awkward and uncomfortable topic my brother and I have ever had. That's really saying something because he is always talking about awkward subjects.

"It's Brenton."

"What's he want?" He asks not even trying to cover the jealousy in his voice. I told him about Breton's confession the other day, about how he still has feelings for me. This didn't sit too well with Garett, he asked me to stop texting him. I did for a couple of days but decided that it wasn't fair for him to text Nichole when I asked him not to.

"Just to talk."

Thankfully he doesn't ask anything more. Instead he gets up and checks his messages on his phone.

"You want to drive to Willits and pick up my cousin, Crystal?"

I have heard so much about her and was looking forward to meeting her.

"A drive would be nice." I say leaving the room to take a shower.

As the warm water pulses over my body, I take the time to enjoy my muscles release all their tension.

Hopefully having another person in the house, especially on he loves hanging out with, will keep him preoccupied enough to stay away from talking to Ashley.

As I open the bathroom door to leave, I smell bacon and eggs. I close the door abruptly shutting out the smell. I rush to the toilet and puke until there's nothing left. Usually it's been anytime I smell pasta or potatoes. I wait for my stomach to settle then take my time to re-brush my teeth as the color comes back to my face. I hurry out to the front yard, careful not to breathe too deeply until I'm outside, with the door closed. I inhale a deep breath of sweet springtime air.

I go to my car Where Adam is checking it out. He asks me to pop the hood so he can make sure everything's fine under there.

"You definitely need a new air filter." He says pulling out the dirty one. He puts it back in and checks the oil and other stuff.

"On your way to Willits, just stop at the auto parts store."

He closes the hood and sends us on our way. I find my way into town with as little help from Garett as possible. We find the small auto parts store with ease.

"Now the hard part is finding the one we need."

Neither of us knew anything about cars or shopping for car parts.

"Maybe we should take this one in so if someone asks we came just show them the one we need."

"Good thinking."

I pop the hood and let him remove the dirty filter. We walk in looking lost.

"How the heck are we supposed to know where to look?"

He heads to the back of the building.

"I'm guessing they're going to be located on the back wall."

Sure enough, he's right. The entire back wall is flooded past the brink with orange boxes depicting various types of filters.

We stare blankly at them.

"I guess we can stand here all day trying to match this up

with the picture on the box, or we can go to the front counter and have someone help us. Take your pick."

He chooses to go ask for help. Good thing too, after the clerk looks up all the part information we were told they didn't have my model in stock and that they would have to order it. They would call me to come pick it up when it comes in. I take my receipt and we head back to the car. I climb into the driver's seat and wait for Garett to replace the filter before starting the car.

After a couple of hours of silence, except for Garett giving me directions, we enter Willits.

"You can stay in the car while I go get her or you can get out and meet everyone."

"I would love to meet them. I'm always hearing stories about them and wonder who they are. It would be nice to finally put faces to the names."

"Turn here." He says pointing out the windshield. I turn abruptly as he tells me to turn again.

I turn and wait for his next direction. We almost reach the end of the gravel road when he yells, "That's it."

I turn sharply and drift to a stop in front of a large mobile house. I take a deep breath and get out of the car. Garett waits for me to reach him before introducing me to everyone as his girlfriend.

I stand there awkwardly feeling everyone stare at me. Jarred sister was there, she just sits there glaring at me. Crystal comes out of the house running and jumps into Garett's arms. She excitedly talks about her new room and offers to show it to him. They begin to walk away not even paying attention to me.

There is no way I'm staying out here on my own. I follow them, keeping close enough to seem included but feeling completely left out all the same.

Her room is a spacious addition away from the rest of the house. We spend a couple of minutes checking out the usual décor of a normal teenager. She shows us around the rest of the house and property. After an hour or so of standing around feeling awkward and out of place, we climb into my car and take off.

Garett asks if he can drive. I gratefully let allow him to, hating how the road winds and curves. He loves to make fun of me for not liking these curves. I tell him I'm not used to driving in circles, Idaho is pretty much a grid compared to this. You can drive in a straight line or a square, not in circles like we do here. Sure it's beautiful how the roads flow with the land but it makes driving a pain in the butt.

Crystal and I crack up laughing as Garett peels out, spraying gravel behind us.

"At least it's not as bad as when we were coming up here. It was horrible."

"She's lying, it wasn't that bad."

Crystal and I spend the rest of the day together bonding. When she and Garett get out a bottle of whiskey, they insist on me taking shots with them. Hesitantly I take one and immediately feel guilty. They continue drinking but I decline anytime the offer me more.

I shouldn't have even taken that one. I'm so ashamed. Maybe I'm just like Garett when it comes to drinking. Every time everyone else was drinking, it made me want some too. I decide to go outside and get away from the temptation.

Brenton texts me, again I ignore him. Finally he calls me; I answer not wanting him to think something is wrong.

"Bloody hell girl, why haven't you answered any of my texts?" I could hear the slight panic in his voice.

"Because I don't feel like getting more lectures from you. I feel bad enough without your help. I haven't told him yet, I don't know when I'm going to but I know it will be today or tomorrow."

"Michelle, you know the longer you wait, the harder it's going to be to tell him. It's going to be okay I promise. If he wants nothing to do with you when you tell him you can always come home. You have people here that would love to have you back. They would want to be there for you especially when you need them the most. I'm sure your mom would like to be close to her daughter at a time like this."

"You make it sound like it's a definite yes. I'm still not

even sure if I'm even carrying his baby."

"You say you don't want to find out on your own, and yet you haven't said a word to anyone but me. You haven't even told him."

"I don't know if I want to find out."

"You have to. You'll find out one way or another."

"I know; I just don't know if I'm ready."

"Ready or not, if it turns out that you are, that baby will come out eventually."

I hang up and decide to sit out front for a while and watch the sunset.

Sean comes out eventually and sits next to me for a while.

"We're going to watch the green mile, you coming?"

I nod my head and stand, following him back inside.

"You shouldn't be alone so much."

Lately I've either been outside on my own or hanging out with Sean. He knew everything that was going on, except for the whole suspected pregnancy part. All he knew was that I was hurting.

"Being alone is sometimes a good thing. It helps me think."

"Thinking is not always a good thing. Sometimes it makes you hurt even more. I want you to be happy. I wish there were some way I could take away all your pain. Maybe if you stop thinking about it so much it won't hurt so badly."

This is much easier said than done.

"How can I not think about it? I still love him more than I can ever say. It's hard to sit back and watch him love someone else."

"That's the problem, he doesn't love her. It's an obsession that has him blinded. He's dumb; he just needs to get over her. She is clear over there in Texas, you're right here. Does that tell you something?"

"It does, it means that I care more and I'm willing to stand by him no matter what happens. I just don't know how much longer I can hold on."

"Does that mean you're leaving soon?"

I can see the pain in his eyes and give him a brief hug.

"I don't know; my family wants me to. My mom wants to fly down here and drive back with me." We watch the movie and continue talking.

"What do you want? Do you want to stay?"

"More than anything. I just want the pain to go away. I want Garett to tell me with his own words what exactly it is he wants. It's emotionally draining trying to guess every day, as if it's a game."

"I completely understand and I know you're tired. Have you talked to him about it?"

So many times, one minute he tells me he's sorry and that we will work things out. The next minute he's ignoring me and choosing Ashley over me. This is what I mean about him treating it like a game. The price to play being my heart.

"I have, he just tells me to have patience. How is that suppose to help me? What is he trying to do? See if he can get with her, and if he can't, fall back into a relationship with me?"

Crystal comes in and lies next to me on the hammock bed to watch the movie with us. She picks up my phone and texts me that Garett went to play his stupid game. We talk some more about how much he has changed

At least I'm not the only one that noticed. His whole family could tell that over the past month he has become someone completely different. Even his best friend, and favorite cousin, who has only been here for less than a day, was already being hurt by him.

She told me how dumb he was being because of the way he's treating me.

He explained the whole break up thing to me. I don't know if I believe what he told me. What happened between you guys?

I don't know, one minute we are happily together, the next he was saying he couldn't be in a relationship. Next thing I know he's texting Ashley, I think they are together but I don't have any proof. Why what did he say to you?

He said he just doesn't love you anymore. Everyone can see that that's not true.

I could feel my heart break even more. Why would he say such things? We all know that it's a lie. Maybe he's just trying to make himself feel better about what he is doing.

When the movie ends I go outside to think to myself I only go back in because I hear Crystal crying loudly. I couldn't talk to her because she was in Mitchell's room talking to him. I had only seen him a few times; once when we were finally introduced two weeks after my arrival. The other times were when he would go make himself something to eat, other than that he would hide away in his room alone. I was told so much about him and how he was terrified of people. He had what most people would call Social anxiety disorder. He would spend his days alone, reading news or playing video games.

I couldn't tell what she was crying about but I could hear her sobs and slurred words as I went to the bedroom. I sit on the bed with Sean and once again look up music videos. Crystal comes in and sits next to me with her tear-stained eyes.

"The first night I meet you, I'm drunk and crying all over the place."

I wrap my arms around her and tell her it's okay to cry.

"I don't mind, I feel like I've known you forever."

She breaks down crying all over again and tells me of the abuse she has to put up with at home. I continue rocking her and reassuring her that everything is going to be okay.

"You're the sweetest person I've ever met. Garett is stupid if he really willing to give you up just like that."

"Crystal!" Garett turns in his chair to tell her to stop.

"She's drunk, leave her alone. If you don't want to hear it then leave." I say trying to defend her.

"You guys love each other. I know it as well as you guys. You just have to get through this rough time but you can still be together I know it."

Garett drops to his knees on the mattress and pulls her away from me.

"Please stop saying that." He says calmly, resting his cheek on her head.

"Why? You know it's true."

He gives her a stern look and she falls silent. She begins to fall asleep in his arms.

"She looks so peaceful. Drunk, but still peaceful."

She wraps her arms around his neck.

"Do you mind if she sleeps in here with us?" He asks picking her up.

I shake my head as he lays her on the bed.

"I'll sleep on the floor; you girls can have the bed."

Crystal sits up and yells at him, not liking this idea. She tells him there is no way he is sleeping on the floor. We all cram together on the twin size mattress; me by the wall, Garett in the middle. Of course this was all a part of her plan. Sometime in the middle of the night, she moves to the floor, leaving me and Garett squished together. I awake with his arm tucked around me and our legs entwined together. This is the first time in a couple of nights that he would even touch me in bed. Most nights he would scoot as close to the edge as possible, careful to leave enough room so there wouldn't be any physical contact whatsoever.

I look up to find Crystal smiling at us.

"Such a pretty picture. This is how it should be."

I watch her leave the room then lay back down, falling asleep in the warmth of his embrace.

CHAPTER 16

Even when I can hear everyone up and about, I can't bring myself to leave the safety and comfort of Garett's arms. The time passes by too quickly, he is the first to get up and leave. I stand up; again the smell of food cooking has me running to the bathroom to puke. I clean myself up and stare at my reflection in the mirror. I talked to Brenton; he said his fiancé might be pregnant. She already had one baby so I figured she would know all about pregnancy symptoms. I told her about the puking in the mornings and the nausea at the smell of potatoes and pasta. She asked how long I've thought I've been pregnant. I told her about two weeks. She told me it was too early for those kinds of symptoms, but then I told her about my dreams.

"They are always with the same little girl. At first she was just insisting that I'm her mother, now that I've accepted her, she interacts with me and Garett in the dreams. Sometimes he goes away for a while, I have a theory about that but I'm sure it's nothing. I can usually see the three of us as a small happy family.

"I don't know what to say Michelle, honestly I think it's too early for symptoms but then again, all pregnancies are different. Maybe you are, Maybe you aren't. Either way I think you should tell Garett and get tested.

"What if he ends up hating my baby?" Thinking I'm pregnant for so long has me thinking I truly am. I have to keep telling myself that there is a chance I could be wrong.

"Then I would say he's a bastard and you need to come home so your family and friends can support you. In the meantime you really need to tell him, especially if you're having dreams like that."

I think of the sweet angelic face of my baby girl. I've come up with a theory for all of Garett's disappearances. The only time he appears in the dreams is when he's not drinking and is his old self. When he's gone, he is being the stupid, drunk, Ashley obsessed Garett.

"I'll tell him soon.

"Good call me or Brenton after you do. We want to be there to help you."

I hang up and go sit outside to think. Sean comes out and sits next to me.

"You okay? You look like you're going to cry."

I hold the tears back and take a deep breath.

"I'm fine. I just need to clear my head."

"You want to talk about it?"

I shake my head and look away from his hurt expression.

"Please let me help. You tell me everything."

He's right; he is the only one here that I tell everything to. Back home the only ones I really ever opened up to were Ashley and Antony. Here Sean became my best friend; he was my advice like Antony, and my shoulder to cry on like Ashley.

"I will let you know soon, I promise. I just need time to think about it alone."

He looks at me with somber eyes.

"Trust me, I'll let you know."

He gives me a hug, holding me for a moment.

"I'll always be here for you."

"I know, thank you."

He gets up and walks away, leaving me with my thoughts. I pick up my phone and call the one person I could talk to about anything, just to have someone listen to me.

"Hello?"

"Ashley?"

"What's the matter?"

"Nothing, I just needed to hear your voice, I miss you. I want to come home."

"You're crying, what happened?"

Sure enough all the tears I've been holding back since last night came flooding out. It's as if the dam built up inside of me finally exploded.

"I have a huge secret to tell you. You can't say anything to anyone living with my mom, please. I don't want her to find out, not yet."

All is silent as she blows her nose.

"Are you pregnant?" Her shaky voice asks.

"Ashley, don't be mad, don't hate me, or think anything bad."

"Are you?"

"I don't know. I think I am."

"Did you take a test? Does Garett know? Does his family?"

"No I haven't taken a test, that's why I'm not sure. I haven't told anyone except you and Brenton. I don't want to stress everyone out, especially if it turns out to be negative."

"Come home"

"I can't."

"You just told me you want to."

"I do want to, but I can't leave. I can't without knowing. If I am, Garett has to have a say, it will be his too."

I've already decided that if I am carrying his child I would stay as long as he wanted a part in the baby's life.

"How long?"

"It's been two weeks since my missed period."

"You're never late. Why haven't you told him?"

"I'm afraid to." I feel ashamed even admitting this. The old Garett I could be sure would be supportive, this new Garett though, who knows how he would react to the news.

"You're going to have to tell him eventually, especially if you are."

I ask her for some advice but she says she can't help me.

"I wish I could, I really do, but how am I suppose to when you're all the way over there?"

"I don't know but I really need you right now. I think I'm going to tell him tomorrow. I could really use your support."

"I'll call you tomorrow then. I have to go and think about all of this."

"Please don't go, I need you now more than ever."

"I'm sorry; this is a lot to take in. Have you talked to Antony?"

"No."

"Maybe you should. I know you don't want anyone over

there to know but he's good with advice and keeping secrets."

She has a point, even though he's two years younger than me, he's done more than I'll ever know. He usually knows exactly what to say and do.

"I'll call him right now"

"Good, call me back tomorrow and let me know how it goes."

I agree and hang up the phone. I wipe away all the tears and steady my voice before dialing. Antony isn't a very calm person when he knows I'm hurting or in trouble. I know I have to keep him calm if I want his help. I don't want his answer to be to come home.

"Hello?"

Good it was him. I don't think I could have kept my voice in check if it was one of my other family members, especially if it was my mother.

"Antony? I need your help."

"What's wrong?"

I guess he knows me better than I thought. I was hoping I was a much better actress. I struggle to keep my emotions hidden but lose, crying so hard I can't stop.

"Michelle, what happened? Did he hurt you?"

"No" I manage between sobs

"What is it then?" he sounds worried.

"I'm s…sorry." I take a minute to control myself.

"Are you pregnant?"

How the heck could they figure it out so easily?

"I don't know"

"How do you not know, either you are or you aren't."

"I don't know, I haven't tested."

I told him about my missed period, the morning sickness, how it's too early for symptoms, and the dreams.

"Man sis you need to get tested. Does Garett know?"

"No I'm too scared to tell him. I had the perfect opportunity but was too selfish and didn't want to ruin the moment."

"Why don't you tell him now?"

"He's mad at me at the moment. I stood up to him, sticking up for his cousin."

Last night Crystal was texting Ashley, telling her not to speak to her cousin anymore, and called her a bunch of dirty names. Garett got mad and yelled at Crystal. Later she was looking at pictures on the phone and he freaked out. He ripped the phone from her hands and yelled at her. He didn't even apologize when he found out she was only looking at the pictures.

"So you haven't told him?"

"I don't want him to think I am making it all up just so he will stay with me."

"He knows you better than that. You're not that kind of girl."

I begin crying again. "I'll tell him soon, I just want everything to be okay. I don't want him to hate the baby just because he doesn't want me anymore."

"That's how it should be. He shouldn't take it all out on an innocent child, especially since its one he helped create."

"Promise me you won't say anything to mom."

He promises and says he has to go to bed so he can get up for school in the morning.

CHAPTER 17

I spend about an hour outside trying to collect my thoughts. I can hear Garett and Crystal giggling through the open window. I go back inside, closing the sliding glass door behind me. Sean meets me with a hug and whispers in my ear, "Feeling better?"

I smile and nod.

"Good, let's go look up some music or ghost videos."

"Okay, but I need to get a drink first."

I head to the kitchen and fill a cup to the top with water from the faucet. I chug it, feeling my dehydrated body soaking it up. I lick my lips tasting the saltiness of my dried tears. Melinda stops me on my way back to the bedroom. She holds a wine bottle in her hand and offers me some.

"No thanks, I'm done drinking."

"Why what's the matter? You're not pregnant are you?"

She says this half out of sarcasm. I think she suspected though, especially since the other night she claimed I was having a girl. I was stunned when she said this and asked her what she meant. She said she saw a little girl hanging on my leg, she was drunk but this still hit home.

"I don't know. I think I am." I say seriously.

She gets a huge smile on her face and puts her arms around me for a hug. "Really?"

I explain everything to her and tell her Garett doesn't know yet.

"I won't say anything then, but I can't believe I might be a grandma. I'm so happy."

She hugs me again and walks away joyfully. I really hope she doesn't say anything.

"I won't say anything either." Crystal says standing two feet away.

We both go to the bedroom and text back and forth so Garett can't hear us. He gets annoyed and goes to take a shower.

Crystal and I begin talking about it out loud. Suddenly

the door opens and Sean steps in.

"What are you guys talking about?" He looks from me to Crystal, expectantly. "Are you finally ready to tell me your big secret?"

Crystal looks at me. I can tell she wants so badly to tell him. I nod my head giving her the okay to spill.

"Michelle's pregnant."

"Maybe." I say as Sean falls to the bed, wrapping his arms around me.

Garett comes in and rudely snaps at crystal about the phone again. I snap back at him which makes him angry. He leaves the room for a couple of minutes to cool off for a minute then comes back when he is calmed.

"I can't do this anymore," He says barely speaking above a whisper. "I can't fight with you or watch you sit back and be depressed anymore." Suddenly he goes silent. "Are you pregnant?"

I was shocked, I was expecting to have to drop the news all on him, and I wasn't expecting him to ask me. I shake my head no.

"Don't lie to him." Crystal says.

He continues staring at me. I lower my eyes and whisper, "I don't know."

Once again I find myself unable to hold back my tears. Unexpectedly he drops to his knees in front of me, wrapping his arms around me, rocking me while I cry.

"That explains a lot. The moodiness, the depression. How long have you been keeping this to yourself? Does anyone else know?"

I nod my head. "Ashley, Antony, Brenton, Your mom, and these two."

"How long?"

"About two and a half weeks."

"Why didn't you tell me?"

I lift my eyes to his, the passion and concern plainly written across his face. I lower my head to hide my shame.

"I was afraid. I didn't want you to think that I made this entire thing up just so you would stay with me. I couldn't keep it to myself anymore, I can't find out on my own. I really need you."

"I know. You're not like other girls. You wouldn't lie about something like this, besides you never said you were. You said you might be; maybe you are, maybe you aren't."

I can't believe he's taking it this well. If I had known it would have been this easy and he would be more excited than angry, I would have said something to him about it weeks ago.

The phone vibrates announcing a text, Probably from Ashley. Garett turns off the phone, not even bothering to check the message, and tosses it across the room onto a pile of laundry. We lay in bed, his arms still wrapped around me. He begins talking about the future.

"Now I really need to get my act together."

"What do you mean?"

"I've got to go to school and get a job so I can support our family."

I can't believe how excited he is. What if I'm wrong? He seems so happy.

"It's not a for sure thing you know. I could be wrong."

He lifts my hands to his lips and kisses them.

"I know, we have to be prepared though, just in case."

"Okay, I just don't want you to get your hopes too high, only to find out that I'm wrong."

My biggest fear now is that I'm not pregnant. I know that most girls in my position would hope for that. After two and a half weeks of keeping it all to myself, I have it in my head and my heart that I am carrying his child, our child.

"I have some rules on how our child should be raised."

"What rules? I could hear his excitement and would listen to anything he proposed as long as it's reasonable.

"Our child can go to church with you but will not be forced to go. Our child can also have a say in what they want to do in life. We will not pressure them to be anything."

I think about this for a minute.

"I think I can live with that."

He smiles and takes a deep breath.

"I'm going to be the best dad the world has ever seen." He begins talking about the future again and all the things he would do once the baby is older.

"I want to name the baby after my dad. If it's a boy, Garett. If it's a girl, Mauricia."

Mauricia, that's beautiful."

Now that angelic girl in my dreams would finally have a name.

"Garett, what if I'm not? I really don't want to let anyone down, your mom seemed really excited when I told her. Now I have you all excited, I really hope I'm not wrong."

"I know. We'll go find out, just don't tell anyone else about it until we find out for sure. Does your mom know?"

"Are you kidding me, she would probably shoot me. Especially if I told her that I'm staying here. None of her grandchildren live anywhere close so she doesn't really get to be a grandma."

"Well we can always go visit."

I smile as he hugs me tightly and kisses me. He whispers about our small family as if he already knows for sure. I fall asleep to his soft, "I love you."

"Daddy, Daddy, Daddy. You came back. I've missed you; please don't go away from us for so long again."

"My precious Mauricia, I'm not going away anymore."

"Ever?"

"Never ever."

"What about mommy? Is she staying too?"

Garett picks her up in his arms and pulls me to them, in our family group hug; I feel all the love seeping from his body.

"We will be together forever and always, a family."

Tears of joy run down my cheeks as he kisses our daughter and holds her close.

The scene changes and I watch as Garett teaches her to ride a bike. He lets go and she falls scrapping her knee. She only stops crying once she is safely in his embrace. The scene changes once more. They both sit in an old rocking chair where he is softly singing her to sleep.

We have our little family, so full of love. Everyone is happy, I have my old Garett back and we both have Mauricia, the love of our lives.

I couldn't be even happier. What had I done to deserve this? For the second time Ashley is out of the picture. I have a feeling she is going to stay that way. The three of us will be left to live out the rest of our adventure in peace.

CHAPTER 18

"Good morning." Garett says as I open my eyes. He kisses my cheek and continues staring at me. He rubs his thumb across my stomach, causing it to do little back flips.

"Sean, Crystal, and Mom know. I'm sure Mom has told Brian by now. That just leaves Mitchell and Nathan to find out. Do you mind if I let Mitchell in on the secret so I can talk to him about it?"

Surely I can't oppose, I have Ashley, Antony and Brenton. It only fair that he gets Mitchell, Brian and Melinda to talk to.

"I don't mind. I'm going to take a shower though, prepare myself for everyone." I wasn't looking forward to having everyone around me, especially since they were bound to be anxious to find out.

Garett kisses my lips briefly, leaving them tingling and wanting more. I watch him leave the room before getting up and heading out to go take my shower.

In the bathroom I look at my naked body in the mirror. Since I've been here I have lost quite a bit of weight. I stick my stomach out as far as possible and rub my hands over it. I don't think I'll be able to handle blowing up like a balloon. Ashley and I used to talk about what our future husbands and kids might be like, what girl hasn't. We would always discuss how we would be there for each other to take care of one another during our pregnancies.

After I shower I decide to call her.

"Did you tell him?" She asks not even bothering to say hello.

"Yeah I told him."

"And?"

"And he's taking it quite well, he's beyond excited. I'm afraid to be wrong, it will crush him."

"I'm sure he'll be happy and overly relieved if you're not."

"He's already picked baby names Ashley. He's already

planning the future. I pray I'm pregnant just so he doesn't get hurt.

"Did you tell him you might be wrong?"

"Of course I did, it doesn't seem like he's listening though. I'm glad to see him so excited, I really am I just don't want him to get his hopes up too high just to find out I'm wrong."

I could tell she was thinking hard as the silence falls between us.

"Has he talked to Ashley about it?"

I smile to myself; I can't help feeling happy and a little proud.

"Nope, he hasn't talked to her since before I broke it to him."

"Wow."

"Yeah, it's like I have my old Garett back again."

"You should have told him a lot sooner. It would have saved you both from a lot of grief."

"I know, I was thinking the same thing. If I would have known he would have taken the news so well, If I would have known he would be more happy about it than angry, I would have said something weeks ago when I first suspected it.

"So does that mean you guys are coming back?"

"No, I can't. I'm staying here."

All of a sudden the tone of her voice changes.

"If you aren't coming back, then what's the point in telling me all this? It's not like I'm ever going to see your baby anyway. What about your mom? Don't you think she would want to play an active role as a grandmother?"

"What about Garett's family?"

"What about them?"

"They're going to be related too."

"So, we are your family, you shouldn't ever choose someone else's family over your own."

Why is she acting like this? I wasn't the one who decided they didn't want me in their house anymore, just because I didn't agree with their house arrest they had me under. I know I left her without saying goodbye and I'm sorry for that, but I still call her every day. She is my best friend, we are supposed to stick up for each other and be there for one another through thick and thin, no matter the distance between us.

"I thought you said you guys were using protection."

"We were, sometimes it doesn't always work. It doesn't help that we didn't use it once, for about ten seconds."

"Didn't you learn in sex Ed that it only takes a second?"

"Please don't lecture me. I just had this conversation with Garett last night when he asked how I could be pregnant when we used condoms. He had forgotten about that one time, it was so long ago."

"Well I still think you should come home."

"I can't Ashley."

"Then why do you call me every day and tell me how you miss everyone and you want to come home?"

"Because I do miss everyone. I miss hanging out with you. I miss being close enough to fight with my brothers when I'm bored. I miss Antony coming up to me for no reason to put his arms around me, just because he wants to dance or pick me up. I even miss my mother constantly nagging at me. I do want to come home but if I do I know things will be exactly the same as when I left."

"How can you possibly know that? Besides it wasn't as bad as you make it seem."

"Oh really, and how would you know? You weren't the one who has been told what to feel.], think, say and do for almost nineteen years. My Mom and I were always fighting and I couldn't stay there anymore. I didn't want to end up resenting her even more than I already did. I love my mom and miss her but I needed to get out. I can't stand being treated like a two year old instead of the responsible adult I always was."

"Well if you're not coming back then there's not much else I can say or do. I really hope you're not pregnant, that will be one of the biggest mistakes of your life."

How can she possibly be saying all of this? She was suppose to be my best friend, she was suppose to be supportive not lecture me and tell me that my child will be a mistake.

"Why would you even say that?" I ask getting angry at her.

"Well it could be that the father is an idiot who yesterday didn't even want you there. Now all of a sudden you could be carrying his child, he wants you again."

"I explained to him that that's not my intention. I don't care if he stays with me. Sure I want him too because I love him more than anything. I just want him to truly be happy. I don't want him to pretend that he wants me just so that we are both there for our child. We could stay as friends raise it together happily. I want him to love me because he wants to, not because I might be pregnant."

Crystal comes out and sits in a green lawn chair. I'm sure she heard the entire conversation but I didn't mind.

"Well I'm going to go. I don't want to see you get hurt, please call me when you find out if you are of not."

I hang up feeling angry with her and even more so with myself. Did I really make it seem like I was using the baby excuse to make Garett happy? My phone rings Breaking into my thoughts. I read the caller ID *Home*.

"Hello?"

"Hey, did you tell him?" Antony's voice comes through the speaker loudly.

"Yeah"

"And?"

"And he's taking it rather well. Actually I'm worried he's getting his hopes up too high. What happens if I'm not? It's going to crush him."

"What do you mean?"

"Let's just say he already has names picked out."

"Really?"

"Yeah. He's so excited, he's scaring me."

"Did you tell him that?"

"No. I told him not to get too excited before finding out."

"So what about his other woman?"

"What about her?"

"Has he said anything to her about it?"

I sit down next to Crystal. Why the heck would she need to know, it none of her business. It's my child not hers.

"I don't know. He hasn't talked to her since last night."

"Before or after you told him?"

"Before, after I told him he turned off the phone, ignoring her texts."

"Well that's a good sign. Did you tell him what you told me about not wanting to tell him in the first place?"

"Yeah."

"What did he say?"

"He said he already knew I'm not like other girls and that I should have told him in the beginning."

"Do his parents know?"

"Yep, his mom tried offering me some more wine. I was feeling guilty for drinking already. I refused and she asked if I was pregnant. She was just messing around and was shocked yet happy when I told her I wasn't sure, but I think so."

"Well that's good that she's supportive. So everyone over there wants you to be?"

"Yep, I think the only one who knows and has a major problem with it is Ashley."

"Yeah I talked to her about it last night."

"I thought I asked you to keep quiet about it."

"I figured you already told her. You tell her everything."

He has a point. I can't really be mad at him, that's a really tough secret to hold on your own, I would know.

"She's only not happy about it because she wants me to come home."

"We all do but I understand that you need to be there right now."

I smile, grateful to have someone on my side who understands.

"Just make sure you come and visit sometimes."

"Don't worry, we will. We've already talked about it."

"Good. I have to go, call me when you find out if you are or not."

"Of course."

"Love you sis."

My eyes fill with tears as I think of his warm smile.

"Love you too."

He hangs up first, leaving me to talk with Crystal. She excitedly tells me about Garett's new attitude and excitement about being a father.

"Please don't egg him on. I need help keeping his hopes down until we find out."

I spend the rest of the day with Garett and Crystal. They both happily drink and I sit back and watch thinking of the day to come. We didn't know if it had been long enough to get tested but we decided to go get a few from the pharmacy tomorrow. Until then I had promised Garett that I was done drinking until I was sure. Of course I had no intentions of drinking anymore; I didn't like the feeling of being drunk anyway. I hated the dizzy and nauseated feeling that come with it.

Eventually, when crystal was so drunk she was about ready to pass out, we decided to go to bed.

Garett lay in the middle, me by the wall again. All night long Garett kept his arm protectively around my stomach. Crystal ended up on the floor again. I'm sure she didn't mind this time seeing as she had so much to drink. Any flat surface would have been comfortable.

CHAPTER 19

Garett kisses my cheek, waking me excitedly.

I pull the blanket up over my head blocking him and the sun out. He dives under the blankets and smiles. I can't help but smile back. The excitement in his eyes reminds me of my little brothers on Christmas morning.

"Good morning beautiful."

"Good morning ugly." He gives me a false hurt look.

"Hey you woke me from a very pleasant dream."

"I'm sorry, you can go back to sleep now if you want."

"Too late, the dreams gone." I push him off the bed then leave the room laughing hysterically.

I quickly take a shower and go to get the tests. Everyone was excited. Melinda gives me advice on which ones to get.

"What if it comes out negative?"

"Then I guess it'll be negative, you can take two just in case. We want to be absolutely sure."

"You guys won't hate me if I'm not?"

"Of course not why would you think that?"

"I don't know, I just don't want people to think that I'm doing all of this to make Garett want to be with me."

"It's not like you lied to anyone. You just said you suspected that you are so now we are going to confirm it." She smiles and hugs me once more before Garett and I head off to town.

I go in, leaving Garett to sit in the car. I didn't need him hovering over me excitedly. Looking all around I don't see any tests out on the shelves. I go to the counter and ask if they sold pregnancy tests. The clerk asks me how many boxes I would like.

"Two please."

She reaches behind the counter and pulls out two different brands.

"These are the last two."

"It's okay, I'll take them."

I wanted to be as accurate as possible. I pay the full

amount with my debit card then head to the car.

Once we get back to the house, I only have one problem.
I can't pee.

"You only need a couple of drops, just enough to cover
the tips." Melinda says anxiously.

I go to the bathroom and try to pee in the small paper cup.
Unable to, I go to the kitchen and chug three large cup of
water.

"Now we wait." I say sitting outside. Ten minutes later I
finally get the urge to pee. I go to the bathroom and fill the
cup halfway. I set it on the counter and open the box of tests.
I read the instructions then dip the tip of the test into the cup.
Garett comes in and looks at my face in the mirror. I set the
stick on the counter, close my eyes and turn around.

As I begin to exit the bathroom, he stops me and pulls me
into his arms. "Everything's going to be okay I promise. If its
positive, well then I guess we will be awesome parents. If, its
negative, at least I'll still have you. Who knows, maybe we
could try again."

I just smile at him and head for the door.

"Now what?" he asks stepping back.

"Now we wait." I go to the living room and sit on the
futon with Crystal.

"Did you find out?"

"Nope not yet. We have to wait a few minutes."

"Are you okay? You don't look so good."

"I'm fine. I'm just nervous."

"Do you want it to be negative or positive?"

After two weeks of thinking I'm carrying a baby, my
body began to believe it. For this reason I wanted it to be
positive. I didn't want Garett to base his relationship and
feelings on this though, for this reason I wanted it to be
negative.

"Both."

"How can you want it to be both?"

I explain my reasoning to her.

"Oh, if it's negative, maybe you and Garett can start over.
If it's positive it's a sign that you guys are suppose to be

together anyway."

I smile as she tries to make me feel better.

I go to check the results but find that the test was malfunctioned. Melinda does the next one for me then excuses us all until it's ready.

"Crystal can you look for me? I don't think I can do it again."

Happily she runs to the bathroom. I watch as Garett goes to the kitchen then came back out with a tall glass of vodka. I watch as he takes a big mouthful and swallows. He closes his eyes to hide his pain.

Crystal comes back looking less excited.

"Well?" I ask my voice cracking.

She shakes her head no. Tears silently fall down my face. She reaches out to me trying to be of comfort. I know I should be happy with the results. Garett wouldn't have to be tied down to a relationship he doesn't want. All I could think about was how a simple answer could make me feel so hollow and empty. I felt like I had lost my child. I know now that there was nothing in me this whole time but I couldn't help feeling like I had lost it anyway. I look back at Garett again, this time I watch as a tear slides down his cheek. He gets up and goes to the bedroom to hide his pain. I follow him hoping I can give him some kind of comfort.

"Garett, I'm sorry." I stand toe to toe with him and try to comfort him. He lays his head on my shoulder, hugging me, and begins to cry uncontrollably. With every sob that wracks his body my heart clenches tighter and tighter in my throat. I begin crying with him.

"I'm sorry; I never should have gotten your hopes up. I tried so hard to get you to remember that it could have turned out negative."

He reassures me that he will be fine. I leave him to gather his thoughts. He spends the rest of the day drinking, Crystal eventually joins him. I take a shot of whiskey and drink a pina colada wine cooler. Deciding I can no longer handle all the disappointed stares, I go sit outside. Sean follows me and tries to cheer me up. Garett watches as I empty the bottle.

"How much have you had to drink?"

"Just that and the shot I had with you guys, Why how much have you had?" He takes the bottle from my hand.

"No more. Tests can be wrong, promise me you won't drink anymore until you know without a doubt." I agree and go sit by myself on the edge of the garden. Why is he doing this to himself? Two tests came back negative, how much more proof did he want? Eventually my period will come and reality will settle in. Crystal and Sean go inside leaving the two of us by ourselves for the first time since this afternoon. He comes and takes a seat next to me.

"You know, I never thought I'd be so disappointed by a negative pregnancy test. I was really looking forward to you having my child." This makes me smile, earlier Sean told me I was still young and Garett and I could try again.

"Maybe it's for the best."

"What do you mean?"

"Look at us. Neither of us have a job, we live with your parents, and we fight every other day. A baby isn't going to fix that."

"Thinking I was going to be a father had me motivated to go to school and do everything else I was supposed to do. Now I don't have that motivation."

"You shouldn't base that on a baby either. You should want to do it for yourself as well."

"When I read the results I felt like my heart had been ripped out. I really did want this; we could have worked everything out."

I begin crying again. If he really wanted this then why weren't we together? If he really wanted this he would stop talking to Ashley and try to fix whatever it is we have left.

"There is always the future."

"No there's not."

"What do you mean?"

"Are you willing to give Ashley up and start building on our relationship? Yeah I'm devastated by the results; I thought I was pregnant for two and a half weeks, which in itself takes an emotional toll on a person. I'm also glad; I don't want you choosing me because of a baby. We could have worked it out. I'm sure we still can but you have to want to." We sit in silence looking up at the stars."You know why I love stars so much?" I ask him trying to relieve the tension.

"Why?"

"Because you can look up at them from just about anywhere at the same time as someone who is far away. It will be like you are looking at them together." Whenever I look at the stars it always makes me wonder what everyone is doing at that moment back home. "Looking at them reminds me that I'm not so far away from those I love."

"You're not going back are you?"

"To visit... soon."

"Good. I don't want you to leave. Mom doesn't either."

I take a deep breath then decide it's time to go inside. Crystal and I text each other back and forth as Garett plays his game and completely ignores us again. He picks up the phone and texts Ashley. We both sit back and watch him for a couple of hours.

I can't believe he's back to ignoring you after all that's happened. He's right back to the drinking and texting that whore, ignoring you.

It's okay, really, I'm used to it.

Garett gets mad and annoyed with us. He decides to sleep on the floor at the foot of the bed, leaving the small mattress to us.

"You shouldn't talk about people behind their back it's rude."

I look at crystal and ask if it's okay to tell him what she wrote. She nods her head and I repeat her words.

"She says she doesn't like what you've become and she wants to go home. You never yelled at her until now. She says she doesn't feel like you love her as much as you used to and she doesn't like who you have become."

He sits up and pulls her to him apologizing. Just then the phone vibrates again signaling a text.

"Why are you still talking to her?" Crystal asks as she reads Ashley's name on his phones home screen.

"Because I love her."

"Why? You're supposed to be with Michelle. She's all the way in Texas why would you talk to her?"

"Because that's what people do when they are dating."

"What about me?" I ask not even bothering to keep the tears out of my voice."

"What about you?"

"So as you said the other night, everything you've said to me has been a lie."

The other night he told me that he lied to me about everything and wanted me to go home. I told him I wasn't leaving and I didn't believe he lied. No one can fake the emotions he used to show me. He then told me that he lied about lying because he was feeling guilty and wanted me to hate him. He couldn't hate me enough to send me away but it would be a whole other story if I chose to leave.

"What about all the stuff you said about wanting me to be the mother of your children?

"I lied just like you lied to me."

"I never lied to you or your family."

"You lied about being pregnant just so I would want to be with you."

Oh no he isn't going there. What the heck is his problem? Why is he doing this?

"Don't you dare! I told you the reasons I didn't want to tell you in the first place. I knew you would throw it back in my face. I am not like other girls, you said so yourself."

"You are just like all the other girls out there. I was wrong. You lied about being pregnant and you've been lying to my entire family, turning them against me. You're a dirty slut that uses men to get what you want and then you manipulate their families and turn them against each other."

"Shut up!" I yell at him. Neither of us had ever told the other this before. It always seemed like the worst thing you could say to someone you loved so much.

"If you really believe that then I'll be leaving tomorrow." I get up to go sleep in the living room.

"When I'm gone you'll see that nothing's changed.

You'll see that your family had to sit back and watch you change into something they don't like. I never lied to anyone; it's been me from beginning to end." I walk across the room trying not to step on him.

"Good! Leave! Everyone here will be much happier when you're gone. All you've been doing is stressing everyone out. Mom hasn't slept in the past two nights because of you."

"Good. I'll be gone tomorrow."

"Good, you say that I've changed, why don't you take a good long look in the mirror. What happened to that good girl that I fell in love with? You changed and became just like everyone else. You think it wont be easy for me to replace you, you're wrong. I'll just go pick up the next whore I see walking down the street."

I reach back to slap him across the face but he catches my hand just before I reach it. I use my other had and feel the sting as it makes contact with his skin. "I should have left a long time ago."

I leave slamming the door behind me. My heart finally snaps the rest of the way, and the tears come rushing to the surface spilling out again.

Sean sits up in bed and asks me what's wrong.

"I'm going home." I manage to sob. He scoots over on his mattress to make room for me.

"Please don't. I don't want you to leave, no one does."

"Garett does. He says I lied to everyone and made them turn against him."

"That's not true. Garett did all this to himself Sure everyone sticks up for you but that's because we all know how much you love him. We can only sit back and watch him throw it all away on a girl who only wants a daddy for her baby. When he was upset after your test this afternoon I could tell he was heartbroken. He wanted a reason to change, a reason to wake up and take responsibility. Now he can sit there and play games and text all day without feeling guilty. If you leave he'll realize what he missed out on."

"Which is another reason I have to go, I can't stay here as long as he thinks I'm lying to everyone. It will only make him resent me even more. I don't want to be here if it's stressing everyone out."

"You're not stressing anyone out. Garett has all that taken care of on his own."

I lay there crying.

"What now?" Mitchell asks annoyed as he comes out of his room.

"I'm going home tomorrow."

"Why now?"

"Garett doesn't want me here anymore."

"Where are you Crystal?"

I dry my eyes on the blanket as he hands me a little stuffed lamb." She's in the bedroom with Garett." Mitchell, thinking I was his cousin awkwardly returns to his room with his stuffed lamb in hand. I was told that it was his most prized possession; he's had it since he was a baby.

"Please don't go." Sean says again. "It would be like losing my big sister."

I hold up my fist and point at my thumb. "You see this; they say a person's fist is as big as their heart. This right here will always be my Sean piece of my heart." He smiles and hugs me.

"Sorry I'm keeping you up all night crying all over you."

"It's okay, what else was I going to do but sleep?" We both laugh.

"I'm going to call my mom, tell her that I'm coming home tomorrow."

"It's two in the morning."

"She'll want to know." I pick up the phone and anxiously dial the number then wait.

"Hello?" My mom's voice sounds sleepy yet worried. I begin crying all over again.

"I want to come home."

"Now?"

"As soon as possible."

She spends twenty minutes trying to calm me down then tells me to wait until the morning before trying to drive home.

"I don't want you staying up all night driving. Get some

sleep then call me when you wake up."

I hang up the phone and crawl back into bed. Crystal tried talking to me while I was on the phone but I waved her off and she returned to the room.

"Michelle…"

I try to hide my tears.

"Go away."

"Please…Michelle."

"Garett, just go away."

I know I should have listened to him. I shouldn't have yelled, but I couldn't talk as long as I was crying. That would only make me feel even more stupid and vulnerable. If only he came out a minute before. I watch regretfully as he walks away, going back into the room. I cry myself to sleep waking hours later to the sound of someone coughing terribly. Thinking its Garett, I go to the kitchen, grab a bottle of water, then go into the room and hand it to him.

"Here I thought you might need this."

He takes it then asks if I would bring him a can of soda. I return minutes later, hand him the can, then return to bed to cry myself back to sleep. Why I did anything for him was beyond me, maybe there was still some part of me that wanted to believe that all this was a nightmare. I wanted to go back in time and be the Michelle and Garett that we were in Idaho. The couple that only needed each other to pass the time; no drugs, no alcohol, and no sex.

CHAPTER 20

"Why is she on the floor?" I hear Melinda ask Sean from the edge of my consciousness. She seemed more worried than she did angry.

"She wasn't there last night, she must have moved off in the middle of the night."

"Why is she even out here, what happened?" Brian asks concerned.

"Garett's a jerk! And she's going back to her family today."

I didn't feel comfortable, them talking about me thinking I'm asleep.

I sit up looking around me.

"Good morning." Melinda smiles at me.

Garett comes out and takes a seat, waiting for Brian and Mitchell. The guys were all going to do a big install today. I just look at him as he stares past me, avoiding my eyes.

Two can play that game. I get up and go take a shower. I'll hang out with Sean and Crystal for a while and then pack all my stuff. I get a call from the auto part store, telling me my air filter has arrived. I decide I can't leave until I get it otherwise it would have been a complete waste of my money.

Crystal and I go into town to get it.

"Melinda isn't going to let you go home alone, I hope you know that. She says Garett has to go with you."

"She shouldn't force him. I don't want him to feel like he has to come. It would make him hate me even more."

"Well she says you aren't going alone, besides maybe if he goes with you, you guys can talk things over and work it all out."

"I think we'd end up killing each other, and I don't know if I really want to be with him anymore."

We stop at the gas station before heading back to the house.

"You should take me with you."

I would be more than happy to but I can't take her from

her family no matter how much they hurt her.

"You have to stay here."

"Why?"

"Because your mom wouldn't let you go two whole states away with nowhere to go."

"I can go to grannies. My mom's going down there in a couple of weeks anyway."

"What about school?"

"What about it? I could miss a couple of days."

A couple of weeks are not just a couple of days. No matter how badly I want her to come I can't take her.

"Schools very important, I can't let you come. You need to stay here. If you want to come down with your mom I'll be more than happy to come and visit."

I can feel her disappointment as we sit in silence the rest of the car ride back to the house.

Now I have nothing to do but wait for Brian to come home and change the filter for me. In the meantime, I toss all my clothes onto my quilt and wrap it up, carrying it to the car.

"Can you please open the door for me?" I ask Sean, struggling to hold all of the edges of the blanket together.

"I really shouldn't, that would be helping you leave when I'm trying to get you to stay."

I give him a sorrow full look. He makes it harder for me every time he says stuff like that. He may not know it but watching him sulk makes the little Sean piece of my heart crack. He opens all the doors for me on the way to the car. He even helps me carry out some of my bags. Once all my stuff is loaded up, I do a walk through of the house making sure I didn't miss anything.

I see Garett's necklace hanging on the door knob, he must have put it there last night when he was drunk. He was always loosing things this way, especially his hat. In the mornings he would usually ask if I had seen it, the response was always, "It's in the room by the bed."

"What are you going to do with that?"

Crystal asks me looking at the necklace with the little golden ring on it.

"I don't know. Its Garett's, I'm not taking it back"

"You should leave it for him where he'll find it for sure."

I lay it on his keyboard. I want to leave a letter to him telling him I'm sorry and that I never meant to hurt him, but I couldn't find any paper and didn't want to bother Melinda for one. I don't know if that was the real reason or if I was hoping that he would know that already. I've told him enough times, it seems kind of pointless saying it one last time.

Even though I was there for over a month, I kept my stuff pretty together. I grab my stuff from the bathroom grateful to have remembered. I tell Melinda and Sean, if they find anything when I'm gone they can either keep it or throw it away.

"You're not leaving yet. Garett brought you here, he is going to take you back and find his own way home."

I wasn't happy about this idea. I didn't want him to feel like he was being forced to come with me. That would only make him resent me all the more. But then again, if he came with me, we would be locked in the car together for twelve hours. That would give us plenty of time to talk.

The guys don't arrive home until about two o'clock, that's three in Idaho. Garett comes into the bedroom where I'm watching TV, waiting.

"Mom says you're not going alone. Either I'm going with you or Mitchell."

"I don't want you to go if you feel like you're being forced."

"Well one of us is going with you."

I leave the room and ask Brian if he will change my air filter before I go. While he does that I decide to call Ashley, she still doesn't know that I'm coming back.

"Hello?" She asks picking up on the third ring.

"Guess what."

"What?"

"I'm coming home." All is silent.

"Did you hear me?"

"Yeah, I heard you; I'm just trying to process it. Don't tell me you're coming unless you're serious."

"I'm dead serious; I'm getting in the car right now and leaving."

She gets excited and tells me she'll let me go so I can hurry and get my butt home.

Mitchell comes out of the house with a couple of pairs of clothes and some toiletries.

This is bound to be one long and awkward car ride. I take turns hugging everyone except Garett,

"I'll miss you guys."

"You don't have to go. You know that." Melinda says glaring at Garett.

I do, if someone thinks I'm turning everyone against him. Besides My little brothers are already excited to see me."

I've had everyone tell me that they didn't want me to leave. Even Nathan was sad. He asked me if I was ever coming back.

"I don't know sweetie, that's up to Garett."

"Why did you lie to me?" he says, his eyes filling with tears.

"What do you mean? I didn't lie to you."

"Yes." He says wiping his eyes. "You said you were staying here forever."

This alone makes me want to go unpack my things and stay. I give him a hug and apologize.

"I'm sorry, I didn't know forever would be so soon."

"Why are you leaving if you love him?"

I don't know how to explain that it takes two people to love enough for me to stay.

"I have to go. I might come back but right now I need my family. Most of all I need my mom."

He looks confused. I close my eyes and try to find a way to explain to him.

"You know how when you're sick or hurt all you need is your mom to make it feel better?"

He nods his head.

"That's why I have to go. Maybe not forever, but for now I need to."

He gives me a hug, understanding that I'm hurt but not understanding why.

"I'll miss you." He says letting go.

"I'll miss you too. Maybe I'll be able to come back and visit sometime." He smiles then goes to play his video game.

Coming here I went through a bit of culture shock. Everyone would sit in separate rooms, or even together and play their own games. It kind of grew on me though. I would definitely miss playing rock-band as a family.

I give hugs to everyone again and go back to Sean for a third.

"You have my number. Text or call me anytime, I love you sis."

I brush a tear away as I nod my head. "I love you too."

Garett watches me say my goodbyes but doesn't move. I want so badly for him to reach out once more and wrap his arms around me. I want him to be the one in my passenger seat. Even more than that I want him to tell me that there's no need for goodbyes for we will be seeing each other again.

I take one last look at this family that has grown so dear to me before climbing in and backing out, heading down the highway towards my home town.

Being locked in the car with Mitchell for twelve hours helped us get to know each other. He was really sweet and reminded me of Garett before the change. We talked mostly about our families and our childhoods. I was surprised when I learned we had so much in common. It's too bad he'll be going back to California; he could be a really good friend. He could help me get over his brother, and I could help him get over his severe social anxiety

Eventually we reached Caldwell, where I dropped him off at his grandmas, then drove down the street to my moms. It was three in the morning by the time I dropped dead tired onto my brothers spacious queen sized bed. To many, it would seem strange for a brother and a sister our age to be sleeping together. I had no place else to sleep except the couch and there was no way I was sleeping by myself. After over a month of sleeping with Garett, I am too afraid of sleeping alone.

I fall asleep the instant my head hit's the pillow. On the way back we had gotten lost twice which extended our trip a couple of hours. I was exhausted but still managed to sleep uneasily.

I stand in the middle of a foggy meadow, unable to see exactly where I am. I have the slight feeling I've been here multiple times before. The pretty purple flowers fade to gray as the mist slowly rolls across them, swirling at my feet.

"Michelle!" I hear Garett's worried voice calling me from somewhere up ahead. I try running, feeling my feet slip and slide on the wet grass. I try to catch up to his voice but am unable to reach him.

I sit up in bed breathing hard, trying to tell myself it was only a dream. For the first time since leaving California, I cry my eyes out. Thankfully Christian already got up and left the room. I didn't want anyone to see me like this. I couldn't let them know that the second I arrived, I regretted coming back. I get up and change into what little clean clothes I have with me, then go to say hello to my anxiously waiting family.

I'm welcomed by all. My mom decided she's going to take us all out for pizza for my first dinner back. After that we are suppose to go to the drive in and see a couple of movies. I call Ashley and invite her but she says she already had plans made.

"We'll go next weekend though, if you still want to." She says apologetically. It is agreed that we would go the following weekend and spend time together with no outside distractions.

At church the following morning, I'm greeted by more anxious people. Some of them I've never spoken to before so it was a little awkward. Alison sees me and runs to me, putting her arms around my neck.

"We're so glad you're home."

I wish I could say the same, all I could think about for the last twenty four hours was Garett, and how much had changed in the short amount of time I was gone..

"I have one question for you." Alison says holding me at

arm's length.

"Is it true you're pregnant?"

Wow word travels fast and far. How the heck would she know; it had to have been Antony, Ashley, or Jarred. Thanks to Melinda telling her mother, Jarred is sure to have heard about my suspicion. I shake my head and ask her who told her. She said she couldn't say and told me over and over again how it was good for me to be back.

I couldn't feel happy about anything. I try to smile but am sure I'm failing miserably. After service ends one of my pastors calls me over to talk.

"I'm sure glad you're back. Since I've been here I've watched you grow to be such an amazing woman with a wonderful smile and such strong faith." I didn't have the heart to tell him that my faith died out for a while and was slowly returning. I not that same amazing woman he knew when I left, its going to take a lot of time and effort to get back to that again.

"I'm not going to lecture you or ask you all that happened while you were down there; I just want to know if you learned anything from your journey?"

I was a little confused by his question; sure I learned a lot of things. I learned that you won't die of a broken heart no matter how badly you wish you could.

I just nod my head, trying to fake another smile.

"Good because if you didn't, you'll have to go back and do it again."

His wife asked me the same thing, only she asked, "What did you learn?"

I'm pretty sure she can see right through my lies and my phony smiles.

"I learned that my family loves me no matter what I do or have done. I also learned that God has never left me, he never does, he just waits for me to ask for his forgiveness."

She talks a bit longer to me about how everyone is so glad to have me home. After another half hour of fake smiles and annoying hugs from everyone, I finally got away. I spend the whole next week sitting by myself, listening to music, staring into space, Thinking back on The last fight I had with Garrett. Most people would say that I'm stupid, or that I'll eventually get over It; I don't think I ever will, even months later it still hurts. Sometimes, just to get away from the pain, I would go to Garett's grandma's house and hang out with Mitchell. We become closer friends than I thought we ever would. He asked me to come back to California with him. At first, I agreed because I knew it would take me closer to The family I had grown to love, maybe I could even work things out with Garett and build a new friendship. I had been texting him, trying to apologize for saying goodbye to everyone but him. He told me it didn't matter and he was with Ashley and better off without me. Soon I found myself becoming attached to Mitchell. I got him out of the house, going for walks or drives every day, he even came to the movies with me for his birthday which surprised me because he wouldn't go anywhere there was a crowd.

The night before we were supposed to be heading back to California, my birthday, my family and I went to the drive in. I hadn't told anyone of my plans except for Antony and Ashley.

Ashley spent the entire night reminiscing with me and told me she couldn't stand it if I left again.

"When you left last time, I hurt everyday you were gone. I knew what I was doing in my daily routines but that's all it was, a routine. My heart was completely absent and I wasn't really into anything anymore. My grades fell and everyone could tell I was different, depressed."

"I can't stay Ashley. I sit here day in and day out thinking of how I could have done things differently. Some days I'm so depressed I feel like just giving up."

"You need to open your eyes to what you have, not what you don't. You have me, you're brothers, everyone at church, and you're mom and step dad, and all the girls at the daycare. Doesn't that mean anything to you?"

"Yes but…"

"If you won't stay for any of us, do it for Mitchell."

"What do you mean?"

She looks at me as if I'm crazy.

"Do you honestly think you're going back because you love him? I don't think so, you're broken. You can't love anyone at the moment because Garett still holds you're heart."

She was a hundred percent right about this. Maybe I was forcing a relationship because I wanted to keep my mind off of the pain. What am I suppose to do? Stay single the rest of my life? I gave Garett my heart, my body, my all. I couldn't get it back no matter how much I wanted it back. The past is set in stone and there's no going back.

Eventually I decided to stay. Ashley is right; it wouldn't be fair for Mitchell to be with me when I was still hurting and somewhat had feelings for his brother. It would cause me to do the same thing to him what Garett did to me with Ashley.

I call Mitchell and let him know that I'm not going back with him. I told him he really is a sweet guy and a good friend, but I just can't go.

"It was easy enough for you to jump in the car and go with Garett. That makes me think you love him more than you love me."

I didn't have the heart to tell him how much I agreed.

"I really am sorry. I didn't mean for anyone to get hurt, especially you." We talk some more, parting as friends.

For the whole of next week, I can't stop thinking of how I could be in California at this very moment.

I don't know what would have happened but I did know, one way or another someone would have been hurt again.

Eventually I began to settle back into my old routines. I would work all day, at the daycare, then go home and be depressed; sitting alone listening to music, thinking of everything I miss In California.

My friends began inviting me to do things with them. I forced myself to go, trying to make my parents think I'm happy. I had to keep my feelings locked up deep in my heart, not letting anyone know that I feel nothing but loneliness and zombie like.

Weeks pass and turn into months, things begin getting

easier for me. I can now talk about Garett without it hurting me so much. I told a couple of my coworkers everything about the time I was away. They all supported me and let me know that the pain would lesson over time. They told me that, because he was my first, he will always be in my heart. I will never lose that love for him, not completely anyway.

One morning I was sitting in the downstairs family room on my bed, also known as the couch, and I couldn't help thinking of the first conversation I had with my pastors when I first got back... I realized that through all the pain, depression, suicidal thoughts, and eventually the road to healing, I learned a lesson. I now fully understand what it is I learned through all of this. Sure I fell in love and had my heart ripped out. I can't say I will never fall for someone else. But in the future, I will stay true to my colors. The drinking, the sex, and the drugs helped me become someone I wasn't. I will never be proud of the things I've done but all I can do is forgive myself and let it go.

One day Garrett will realize he has a problem, he might also see that he is missing out on the greatest love he will ever find. I just hope he opens his eyes before it's too late. Do I regret any of the pain and suffering? No, because without it, I would never have known the love and joy I once had with him. People often ask me if I could, would I go back and change anything in the time I was gone. I simply smile at them and say, "I learned a lesson, I'm sure you can apply it to your life as well. It has taught me to keep moving ahead, no matter how great the pain or struggle; things will work out in the end. The most important thing I want you to remember is, good or bad whatever we do today shapes our tomorrows. Our choices make up who we are each and every day. Things may seem wrong at the time but in the end all wrongs will right themselves. Live with no regrets. Live so you can laugh at little things and enjoy the beauty in life, until someone stops you and asks 'are you high?' You can smile back at them and say, 'High on life.'"

****

EPILOGUE

I'm sure that many people can relate to a story such as this. If you know of someone who is hurting and needs some words of encouragement, talk to them. If you have a friend or a loved one that abuses drugs and alcohol, show them that life can be much better than all that. Even if they seem like they aren't listening tell them how much you care, they will hear you. Let them know that it's all a part of their journey to finding love and that their story isn't over; for no story ever truly ends...

SPECIAL THANKS

I want to thank my mom and step dad for all of their love and support, and my brothers for their patience with me as I holed myself up in the office not noticing anyone. I especially want to thank Danielle I know how hard this has been on you. Take a deep breath, release all the tension and let's begin our adventure one day at a time. Thanks girls (and Cody) for keeping me motivated, without you guys this book wouldn't have even reached the middle.

www.ingramcontent.com/pod-product-compliance
Lightning Source LLC
Chambersburg PA
CBHW022125170626
46808CB00002B/840